A Happy English Child

By Ursula Zilinsky

A HAPPY ENGLISH CHILD
THE LONG AFTERNOON
MIDDLE GROUND
BEFORE THE GLORY ENDED

A Happy English Child

URSULA ZILINSKY

PUBLISHED FOR THE CRIME CLUB BY
Doubleday
NEW YORK
1988

All of the characters in this book
are fictitious, and any resemblance
to actual persons, living or dead,
is purely coincidental.

Library of Congress Cataloging-in-Publication Data
Zilinsky, Ursula.
A happy English child / Ursula Zilinsky. -- 1st ed.
p.   cm.
ISBN 0-385-24322-7
I. Title.
PS3576.I46H3 1988   87-21935
813'.54--dc19   CIP

Copyright © 1988 by Ursula Zilinsky
All Rights Reserved
Printed in the United States of America
First Edition

For my favorite OAP

A Happy English Child

CHAPTER I

In the dressing room of the Rigby Repertory Theater, Algernon Jagat half filled King Claudius's goblet with Bombay gin, then carefully added a single drop of vermouth. The quantity of gin was calculated to let him swallow the maximum amount of drink while, in the role of Claudius, appearing to be desperately rejecting the poisoned wine forced upon him by Hamlet. Much as he longed for it, he was always very good about not drinking before a performance, or indeed during it, until his last scene, so this would be the first cocktail of the day. He could hardly wait.

The dressing room was very quiet. Bertie de Grey, still in his Polonius costume, but set at liberty by Hamlet's dagger, was napping on a ratty sofa relegated to the dressing room when it had outlived its usefulness as a stage prop. Rosencrantz, Guildenstern and Ophelia were at the pub next door, from where the assistant stage manager would fetch them in time to take their curtain calls.

Even in the unforgiving light of the make-up mirror, Algernon Jagat's face was flawlessly, flamboyantly handsome; a face, he thought, not for the first time, which ought to have guaranteed success in a profession where looks counted for so much. Of course, if he had been English instead of Indian . . . His dear parents had done everything that could be done with money to make him so. The name Algernon with its Wildean echoes of a long gone aristocracy ("Half of the chaps who get into Bankruptcy Court are called Algernon . . .") English tutors, a nearly first-rate public school, Oxford. But none of it had deceived the English. A face formed for a *jeune premier,* a young lover and hero, was also the face of a lesser breed, and politely and quietly it had been brought home to him that heroes and lovers are always white.

His one big success had been a recent television production of *Dracula*. Television still cast its actors on the old principle that niggers begin at Calais, and it did not boggle at the notion that India was a long way from the Count's home in Transylvania. But in spite of his success as the blood-swigging Dracula, he was out of work more often than in, and when his old friend John Silk had offered him an engagement for the summer season at the Rigby Rep, he had reluctantly accepted. Yorkshire was not his idea of a place, and a small repertory theater hardly his idea of a job, but he needed the money. Timothy Selkirk, the current youth in his life, was not a gold digger in the accepted sense of platinum cigarette cases and silk shirts—he did not smoke cigarettes and his clothes were the merest rags—but the stuff he did smoke, as well as the yellow, red and blue pills he swallowed with such abandon, were far from cheap. And the rags he wore, Algernon had discovered, cost a pretty penny when bought on Carnaby Street.

This amiable if vague youth had once expressed the idea of wanting to become an actor (unless, of course, he suddenly turned into a rock star, or went to the Himalayas in a van with some people he knew) and had been pleased when Algernon succeeded in getting him a small part as a page in *Hamlet*.

"You won't need to do much, just swell a progress, start a scene or two," Algernon had reassured him, though Tim had voiced no anxiety. It had not surprised Algernon that he did not recognize the quotation—he had been educated in California and never recognized any quotations—but he did find it odd that someone who, however vaguely, wanted to be an actor, had never read Eliot or *Hamlet*.

An icy draft knifed its way through the ill-fitting dressing room door. Algernon shivered despite the heavy cloak which was part of his Claudius costume. "Rigby, oh my God," he muttered—Ally Jagat playing the 1970 Rigby summer season and grateful for the work. Christ! To cheer himself up he took a swig straight from the gin bottle. In the mirror he saw that Polonius had opened one eye, and was watching him. It was a look of such malevolence that Algernon jammed the cork back into the gin and pushed the bottle as deeply as it would go into the pocket of his raincoat. Bertie de Grey closed his eye and went back to sleep. Slack-jawed, wrinkled like a tortoise, he looked, despite Polonius's robes of state, exactly what he was—a sodden, drunk, over-the-hill old actor.

Yet his was a name to stir memories, to bring back at its mere mention the chills and goose bumps experienced years ago at one of his breathtaking performances. Even now there were times, brief moments when, like an old clockwork toy jogged into life by a careless foot, a line or a gesture could bring back the incandescent Bertie de Grey of thirty years ago. But drink had a long time ago done for Bertie as it would probably, thought Algernon, do for him. Perhaps John Silk had hired Bertie as a horrid example. It was dear of him, if so. But then, Johnny was a dear. Pity that horrible examples so rarely worked.

Algernon looked at his watch and checked his make-up. Grease paint had flattened the distinctive arch of brow and cheekbones, and had fleshed out the jowls and lips. "Ally doesn't act," Bertie de Grey liked to say with a sneering glance at the Cecil Beaton photograph tucked into the frame of the make-up mirror, "he just has cheekbones."

Ah, but dear Cecil had known how to value them, how to use light and shadow to bring out the exquisite hollows of brow and jaw, the straight eyebrows starting low over the bridge of the nose and slanting toward the temples.

Getting ready to return to the stage, Algernon went through a series of stretching and loosening-up exercises, in the course of which he tore a seam in his cloak. It was the same seam he had torn two days before, and Mrs. Shrubsole, the wardrobe mistress, would be cross. Though really it was her fault, since she always cobbled seams together with gigantic stitches and never tied anything off properly. John Silk said she was the worst wardrobe mistress he had ever been cursed with, as well as the most disagreeable, but the Union would not allow him to get rid of her.

Algernon wondered whether he could mend the rip with cello-tape, but it was large and in a vulnerable position, and might give on the stage. He put on his most charming smile and went to the stuffy little room where Mrs. Shrubsole presided over the costumes. She was watching the umpteenth rerun of *The Wives of Henry VIII*, drinking tea with her sister-in-law Mary Barnes, the cleaning woman, and doing no work whatever. Being caught idle did not disconcert her. The expression on her face showed very clearly that she resented being interrupted in doing nothing.

Smiling winsomely, Algernon held up the sleeve to show the tear, and watched the thread-thin lips disappear in a show of annoyance. She was Mrs. Shrubsole, not Miss, and he wondered what her husband could be like. Or were wardrobe women called "Mrs." for the sake of respectability, like Victorian cooks? It was impossible to imagine any man wanting to get under her skirts. Ally found himself smiling at the very thought, and Mrs. Shrubsole, who was licking the end of a thread as if the task would be the death of her, looked at him as if she had read his mind. Hastily Algernon turned his eyes to the little figures posturing on the screen. He had played a Spanish ambassador in one of the early episodes (wogs, as always, beginning at Calais). He said placatingly, "You would have been interested in the wardrobe of that production, Mrs. S. It was all done on a shoestring, you know, polyester furs and rabbit tails dipped in ink, and all those chains of office were plumbing washers strung together."

Mrs. Shrubsole did not answer. She had, as he well knew,

no interest at all in her trade, and did it only for love of the pay envelope at the end of the week.

When Mrs. Shrubsole had cobbled the tear together with stitches so large he knew it would inevitably come apart again before long, she handed the cloak back to him and returned her attention to Henry VIII. There, thought Algernon, was a man who would have known how to deal with Mrs. Shrubsole.

Algernon practiced charm as automatically as he breathed. He wasted another smile and said, "Thank you, Mrs. S., you're an angel of mercy," and patted her where he vaguely thought women appreciated a friendly pat. "Bloody wog," Mrs. Shrubsole muttered under her breath before he was quite out of earshot. Odd, he thought, that no matter how much one considered the source, incidents like this were never entirely painless.

He had only a few minutes left before the scene change and looked around for Verity Barnes, the prop girl. Verity, who thought him the living end (indeed, she had a copy of the Cecil Beaton photograph hidden in her bedroom) smiled at his approach. He gave her his very best smile in return. The most un-English thing about him was his teeth. They were large, even, and all his own.

Verity had a vivid memory of him as Dracula. "Mr. Jagat makes it abundantly clear," a reviewer had written at the time, "that those vampire fangs are the Victorian euphemism for the male sexual organ."

Honestly, Verity thought, her clear skin coloring at the memory, the things they put in the papers sometimes. But the recollection of those fangs did not keep her from returning his smile. Of course, he wasn't wearing them now, and they said he didn't fancy girls. Actors were funny that way. Either they were absolute wolves, their hands all over the place, or else they were—well, you know. Luckily for Verity, who was an old-fashioned girl and intended to present herself intact at the marriage bed, most of the actors at the Rigby Rep were of the second sort.

Algernon said, "What a pretty jersey, love. You should always wear pink. It matches your cheeks. Listen, Verity, my dear, you see this goblet? That is mine. It must be put on the right-hand side of the table. Last time you put it on the left and Gertrude took it instead of her own. Now, I will not conceal from you, Verity, my dear, that mine has a tiny tot of gin in it. *Hamlet* is a very exhausting play and I must keep up my strength. But Miss Wood is AA and must not touch liquor in any shape or form. There is a great deal to be said for sobriety, she tells me, though I don't see how any of it can ever make up for a really nice gin and French, but you do see, Verity love, that we can't have her hoist her goblet, say, 'The Queen carouses to thy fortune, Hamlet, Crikey, it's gin,' and spit."

Verity was about to say that she was ever so sorry, but Algernon did not give her the chance. "Yes, I know, darling, it brought down the house, but that isn't exactly what one wants at the end of *Hamlet*. So you will be very, very careful, won't you."

"Oh, I promise I will, Mr. Jagat," Verity said earnestly.

"Ta, love," said Algernon, giving her a pat in the same general area where he had patted Mrs. Shrubsole, but with far more gratifying results. Gavin Beauclerc, in a great sweat after his difficult graveyard scene, observed this as he came off stage, and whispered, "I should be careful, Sweetie, or she'll end up between your sheets one fine night and then where will you be?"

The scene changes were quick—Hamlet and Osric, Hamlet and a lord, Hamlet alone with Horatio, being philosophical about Providence and sparrows—then the curtain came down and Gavin, who had attended a quick birthday celebration of a fellow actor during the interval in the Theater Pub, and had foolishly downed a pint of ale, made a rapid dash toward the lavatory. John Silk, the manager and director of the Rigby Rep, smiled at his Hamlet's abrupt sortie and said to Algernon, "Such a nuisance, with tights. Well, at least he has the comfort of knowing we can't start without him. Has anyone seen Barnes? Oh, there you are."

The theater carpenter wore an apron with a kangaroo pocket filled with tools. He touched the rim of the cap he wore indoors as well as out because the drafts of the theater chilled his balding head. "Barnes," said John Silk, "the lights went out again during rehearsal this afternoon. Could you have a look at the fuses before you go home?"

At the very moment he finished speaking, all of backstage was plunged into darkness. Verity Barnes was heard saying, "Oh, please be careful," as someone jostled the table with the goblets on it, which she and her mother had been about to carry on stage.

"The phantom heard you, Johnny," said Algernon in the dark. "Don't you know that talking about the electricity backstage is as unlucky as mentioning *Macbeth?*" Matches and cigarette lighters flared, creating unhelpful pools of light in the darkness. Barnes, who always knew where the one flashlight with live batteries could be found, said, " 'S all right, I'll see to her," and went unhurriedly off to the fusebox. The actors remained in the dark, quite accustomed to such incidents, for the theater was very old and the electric wiring a disgrace. Money for replacement was hard to come by, and since the building stood under the loving but stern protection of the Georgian Society, permission to make alterations and improvements usually took so long to obtain that whatever money John Silk had managed to set aside had to be spent on some other, more pressing emergency.

"I say, Johnny," said Gavin, lighting his way back from the lavatory with a match, "Mick and Tim are in the loo, being fearfully sick. Heaven alone knows what they've been experimenting with this time."

"Oh dear," said Algernon, Tim being his temporary possession and therefore responsibility. "I do wish he wouldn't."

"I told them to keep out of sight. Talk about grim death. Ah, light!"

Everyone blinked in the sudden brightness. Mrs. Barnes and Verity hurriedly carried the table with the goblets on stage. Verity sniffed the contents to make sure Mr. Jagat had his gin and French. She thought it a very nasty smell indeed. The lights in the house went off. Mrs. Barnes, giving a final flick at a speck of dust with her overall, was nearly caught on the scene as the curtain rose. The house lights were on a separate circuit and had not gone out when the backstage lights had failed. So quickly had Barnes repaired the fuses that it was unlikely, John Silk thought, that anyone out front had noticed anything amiss. All the same he decided to go around to the back of the auditorium to make sure everything was all right. He always enjoyed watching part of the play with the audience, guessing at their reactions. On an evening like this, when Old Age Pensioners got in for half price, there was of course no need to guess. Like children they voiced their pleasures and displeasures, having no idea, poor deaf darlings, how clearly their comments carried.

Hamlet and Laertes talked and talked. Algernon, no doubt wanting his drink, said, "Give them the foils, young Osric," with a touch of impatience which pleased the audience, who were hoping to have time for a quick one at the pub before closing time, and felt that if not stopped, Hamlet and Laertes might talk all night. "Set me the stoups of wine upon that table," Algernon grandly commanded, though they were already there, and both he and Gertrude had a quick look to see that everything was where it should be.

Hamlet and Laertes fenced, very fast and gracefully. John Silk was particularly good at directing scenes with quick, tight movements, and Gavin Beauclerc was a beautiful fencer. For a moment the audience was caught up in the scene and forgot about the pub and closing time. The queen, offering wine to Hamlet, reminded them, and several people looked quite openly at their watches. Hamlet refused the drink, which put the audience against him. Having watched five acts they had worked up a powerful thirst. Hamlet and Laertes fell to fencing again. The queen, despite Claudius's warning, took a nip of wine, and after some more fencing fell writhing to the floor.

"She's not got a very strong 'ead," Mr. Oakroyd muttered to his wife.

"Shsh," Mrs. Oakroyd hissed. "It's poisoned."

Must have got it from the Theater Pub next door, thought Mr. Oakroyd. All wind and water, their beer was. But there'd never be time to get to White Hart where a man could have a decent pint of Biggle's Golden Ale. His wife overflowed her seat on one side of him, while her sister Enid billowed on his other. Very big on culture those two were, as well as in body. Now that they were OAPs and could get cheap tickets, there was nothing those two wouldn't go and see.

Matters on stage had moved along during Mr. Oakroyd's brief meditation. Hamlet had the King by the throat and was pouring poisoned wine into his mouth. King Claudius doubled up and groaned terribly. Even such cultured members of the audience as Ethel and Enid did not at once realize that anything was amiss. If they thought Claudius's death convulsions were overly dramatic as well as indelicate, well, Mr. Jagat was a foreigner, and foreigners were known to be very emotional.

It was from the stunned looks on the faces of the other actors that the audience slowly began to grasp that something was not right. Then the curtain was hastily dropped, as a murmur of conjecture rose from the stalls. John Silk hurried backstage, and in a moment the audience had the exquisite pleasure of seeing him step in front of the curtain and ask whether there was a doctor in the house.

There proved to be a young medical student, who could

hardly believe his luck. Smoothing his hair, and feeling every eye upon him, he calmly and gracefully made his way up the aisle and was guided onstage by John Silk.

He could see at a glance that King Claudius was dead. There was no pulse, no response at all. Dark splotches had begun to form on Algernon Jagat's face. The young medical student looked up at the other actors. "What happened?"

The actors were either standing about looking stunned, or ministering to one of the pages, who was behaving very strangely, rocking back and forth on his knees, muttering, "Oh man, oh wow, oh Jesus," over and over again.

John Silk said, "What did happen, Gavin?"

The young actor who played Hamlet looked very shaken. He had known, of course, that there was always gin in Algernon's goblet, and that while the king made feeble gestures to push the cup away, Ally had gobbled as much of it as he could get. It had become an affectionate joke between them, for the younger man had admired Algernon as an actor and liked him as a person, as indeed everyone but Mrs. Shrubsole had.

He said, "I don't know, really. I mean I knew there was gin in the cup, but I don't know what happened after that. He got an extraordinary look on his face and clutched his throat—at first I thought it was a joke, we did rag about sometimes—sorry, Johnny, but you know how dull *Hamlet* can get—but of course when he began to roll on the floor and made all that noise I knew something was very wrong. Ally wouldn't have done anything to spoil a scene. Did he have a heart attack, do you think?"

The young medical student had picked up the goblet and was sniffing it. Never in his entire life had he hoped for something as exciting as this. Waiting till every eye on stage was on him (an actor manqué, John Silk could not help thinking) he carefully put down the goblet and said, "Please, no one touch anything." He turned to John Silk. "I think you'd better send for the police. I may be mistaken, but I think Mr. Jagat died of arsenic poisoning."

John always, afterward, remembered the faces of the other actors, like fish behind glass, stupid with shock. Ally's boy was still rocking back and forth, chanting his quiet, silly litany, "Oh man, oh wow, oh Jesus . . ." No one else said anything.

In the silence John became aware of a rising murmur on the other side of the curtain. Silly clots, he thought, why didn't they go home? But of course, being Yorkshire, they wouldn't leave a seat they'd paid for until they'd squeezed the last drop of drama from the evening.

He asked Gavin to telephone the police, while he himself stepped once more before the curtain, and holding up his hand for silence, said, "Ladies and gentlemen. I am extremely sorry to have to tell you that Mr. Jagat, whose performance as King Claudius has thrilled us all, has been taken seriously ill. We shall be grateful if you will all leave quietly, and we hope to have the pleasure of seeing you again soon."

"What about your money being cheerfully refunded at the door," asked a belligerent voice from the audience.

"Yes," said Ethel Oakroyd, just as loudly. "Though why they can't finish the play I don't know. Claudius would be dead by now anyhow."

Some people were doing as John had asked, leaving quietly and politely, but they were mostly the scientists and their wives from the hush-hush genetic research place ten miles out of town. Most of them were Londoners, the kind of people who did not mind how they threw their money about. The locals were made of sterner stuff and sat on as if their bottoms had been poured in cement.

"Yes, let's have the end of the play," shouted Enid, seconding her sister. Several of her cultured friends said, "Hear, hear." "Let's 'ave our money back," shouted Mr. Oakroyd, who knew it was now too late for the White Hart, and wished to extract some small profit from the evening.

John Silk, who operated the theater on a very strict budget indeed, had no intention of refunding the ticket money. They'd had two hours and fifty minutes of a three-hour play, and had one devil of a nerve to ask for their money back. He said, "Please, ladies and gentlemen, the play was nearly over."

"We've got more coming," said Ethel Oakroyd.

"We paid for the 'ole *'amlet,*" said Enid, and a chorus of cultural handmaidens agreed.

Oh no you haven't, thought John Silk. The whole *Hamlet* takes five hours. Your bladders, my old dears, could never take it. But he was really fond of his OAPs, who, simply because it was half price, had so ardently embraced culture late in life. "I'll tell you how it all ends," he said, coaxing them as if they were children, and before either Ethel or Enid could object that they had paid for a full complement of actors, costumes and scenery, he plunged directly into the complications of the plot; he became Laertes beseeching forgiveness, Hamlet enjoining Horatio to absent himself from felicity, and died at last, the rest being not silence, but the noisy arrival of Fortinbras. The audience, putty in the hands of an experienced actor, forgot about refunds and pubs, and left as quietly and politely as, some time before, they had been requested to do.

John stepped behind the curtain and lit a cigarette. His hands shook, and he could feel his shirt, cold and clammy, cling to his shoulder blades. He had deliberately kept his mind away from the image of his friend lying on the floor, but his body had remembered and now exacted payment.

The stage was empty, except for Gavin, still in costume, and the body of Algernon, covered by a blanket, awaiting, Gavin said, removal by the Scarborough police ambulance. "I didn't quite like to leave him," he said. "I know it can't matter to him now, but . . ."

"Yes. Thank you, Gavin. Has the police come yet?"

"Gaskell and Troutt," said Gavin, referring to the local

constables. "Gaskell's in the green room, interviewing people. Troutt's telephoning, I think. An inspector's coming from Scarborough with the ambulance."

Constable Troutt, who, strictly speaking, should not have left the body, returned to the stage and was glad to see some company. Being there with the corpse gave him the willies. Rigby was a quiet town. Directing traffic on market day, dealing with the occasional drunk and returning lost umbrellas to their owners, was the range of his usual duties. Sudden and violent death, while very interesting on the telly, was not really in his line, and he did not like it.

When the ambulance arrived, John Silk and Gavin went to the green room, where Constable Gaskell, very full of his own importance, was taking down depositions. The actors, crowded into the small room, were plainly in a state of shock. Those especially who had been on stage with Ally when he died were white and sick. And no wonder, thought John. Actors, like Shakespeare's cowards, die many times before their deaths, and do so in a great variety of ways, but it was not likely that any of them had ever encountered the real thing, with its failure of bowel and bladder, its fall of blood. John, who had toured the Far East with ENSA during the war, had seen enough of death not to be horrified any longer, but he well remembered his first time, and sympathized with his actors.

Someone had made a pot of tea, but no one, it seemed, had touched it, remembering, no doubt, the poison in Ally's gin. Yet they all looked as if they could do with something hot.

John decided it was his duty to take charge. "Oh, splendid," he said, his well-trained voice betraying no hesitation. "Tea!" He poured himself a cup and drank it. When he did not fall down dead, or even double up with cramps, the others gathered gratefully around Nell Wood, who, still in her Queen Gertrude costume, began to pour out for everyone.

Detective Inspector Winterkill, who had come over from

Scarborough, now came into the green room and introduced himself. He was a man in his mid-forties, whose longish hair and Nehru jacket betokened the fact that he had not come to terms with middle age. John longed to tell him in pure kindness that bell-bottom trousers were a mistake on a man who had failed to keep his figure.

Constable Gaskell handed over several pages of notes, explaining that he had been trying to get an idea of where everyone had stood during the duelling scene. Polonius had been asleep in his dressing room, Rosencrantz and Guildenstern . . .

The inspector had spent the afternoon judging a children's pet show at the RSPCA fête (first prize: Timmy Sneaton—hamster), and the evening catching up on his paperwork. He had been just about to settle down in the big armchair with his wife, who for a wonder had not clamored to be taken either to the pub or the Budgie Cage to dance, when the telephone had rung to summon him to put his shoes back on and come to Rigby to deal with a murder at the Rep. He was therefore in no mood to tolerate Constable Gaskell's officiousness, and told him quite sharply that it was the inspector's job to take down depositions. A constable's sole duty, he reminded Gaskell, was to remain with the corpse to see that nothing was touched or removed.

"You might start looking for a bottle or a scrap of paper that might have contained the poison," he said, enjoying the look of dismay on the constable's face at the thought of this impossible task. "And now," he said, "if you will all be so kind as to tell me where you were during the duelling scene." He turned to Bertie de Grey, as the eldest of the group, and wrote down his name: *Bartie de Grey.*

"No, no, no," Bertie said testily. "B-E-R-T-I-E."

"It's spelled Bertie and pronounced Bartie," said John Silk before either the inspector or his Polonius could explode.

"I see. Thank you." Feeling a certain loss of grip, the inspector turned back to the old gentleman in his Polonius

A Happy English Child

costume and said, "If you will tell me where you were during the duelling scene, sir . . ."

"I was dozing in my dressing room."

"Any witnesses to that?"

"Well, yes," said Bertie, giving a muted actor's cough. "Yes, my dear chap. The—ahem—deceased, I believe is the correct term."

Inspector Winterkill, thinking, Christ, you'd make a lovely suspect, said, "Did you leave the dressing room at any time while the duelling scene was going on?"

"My dear," Bertie told him wearily, "have I not just told you I was dozing? Unless, of course, you confuse me with Lady Macbeth and think I was sleepwalking."

"We only have your word for the fact that you were dozing."

"Alas," said Bertie in his grandest manner, "the dead cannot speak and so cannot bear witness."

Inspector Winterkill turned to the others with considerable relief. Rosencrantz, Guildenstern and Ophelia said they had waited for the end of the play at the Theater Pub next door. Nell Wood had been on stage, as had Gavin Beauclerc, Nigel Pratt and any number of attendants and footmen. Tim Selkirk and his pal Mick Carmody had been in the loo being extremely sick, to the authenticity of which there were several witnesses. Verity Barnes, their prop girl, Nell explained, had been so horrified by Algernon's death that she had given way to a mild fit of hysterics, and had been taken to lie down in the dressing room Ophelia and Nell shared. Her mother was looking after her.

Mrs. Shrubsole assured the inspector that when she had seen Mr. Jagat just before his final scene, he had shown no signs of distress either gastric or mental.

"What happened then?" the inspector asked.

"A fuse blew as everyone was waiting to go on," John Silk said. "It happens all the time. Luckily Barnes, our stage carpenter, is very good with electrical things, so he was able to repair it quite quickly. When the lights came back, Mrs. B. and Verity carried the little table with the goblets on stage, and everyone lined up and marched on in a stately and dignified manner."

"Mrs. Bee?"

"Oh, sorry. Mrs. Barnes, Verity's mother. She cleans the theater."

Was it usual, the inspector asked, for her to be at the theater so early.

This question enraged Mrs. Shrubsole. "Yes indeed, it was usual for Mrs. Barnes to be here early," she said, turning on the inspector as if he had impugned her chastity. Mrs. Barnes often stopped in to have a cup of tea and a natter with her, they were sisters-in-law, and if the inspector thought there was something wrong with that, she would like to inform him that a tea break was part of her contract and anyone who said it wasn't could check with t'Union.

If there was one thing John Silk disliked more than Mrs. Shrubsole's temper, it was having "t'Union" down on him, so he hastened to soothe her, assuring her that she was of course perfectly entitled to her tea break, and to have it with whomever she chose. Inspector Winterkill turned to Gavin and asked him whether anyone on stage would have been able to put the poison into Algernon Jagat's goblet. Poor Gavin looked very pale, and no wonder, thought John. It had been he, after all, who had, however unwittingly, forced the poison down poor Ally's throat.

"Technically, I suppose, someone could have," he said with a nervous yawn. "But it would have been chancy, in plain sight of everyone."

"Do actors actually drink at such times?" the inspector asked. "I'd always assumed it was pretense."

"Quite often it is, or else it's tea or something innocuous," John said. "But poor Ally always had his first gin of the day during that scene—he was very good about not drinking before a performance—so of course he did swallow what was in the goblet. It was a kind of joke around the theater. Everyone knew. He and Gavin worked it out so that it looked as if Hamlet were forcing him to drink while he was actually enjoying his martini."

The inspector wouldn't have minded having a drink himself. Constable Gaskell came into the room, carrying a large waste basket. He said he had found a great deal of rubbish—chocolate wrappers, cigarette packets and such—which might conceivably have contained the poison, but there was nothing to show that any of it had. The boys at County Forensic would have to check it out, he said, smiling, knowing how popular such a request would be. Mrs. Shrubsole looked at the basket with distaste and asked of no one in particular how much longer they would have to stay. She was a hardworking woman, she told the air, who needed her sleep. The inspector, who was happy to be rid of Mrs. Shrubsole, told her she could go. "I don't see any reason why Verity and Mrs. Barnes shouldn't go as well," he said, knowing that they were locals and not likely to decamp, even should they prove to be guilty. Ophelia, who had a car, offered to drive Verity and Mrs. Barnes home if the inspector did not need her any more. Since she, Rosencrantz and Guildenstern had been at the pub at the time of the murder, Inspector Winterkill said they might go too. Constable Gaskell, hardly able to believe his luck at catching the inspector in a mistake, cleared his throat and said, "Excuse me, sir."

"Yes, Gaskell, what is it?"

"Sir, it's true the lady and the two gentlemen have an alibi for the time the poisoning occurred. But isn't it possible that the poison wasn't put into Mr. Jagat's goblet? Couldn't it have been in the gin bottle all along?"

Inspector Winterkill felt himself going hot with embarrassment at having overlooked so obvious a possibility, and anger at having it pointed out to him in front of everyone by Gaskell. He kept his temper under control with difficulty.

"Well, make sure the bottle's sent to the lab," he said. "And mind you don't get your fingerprints all over it."

Constable Gaskell, who had only just thought of the possibility, had to admit that he did not have the bottle. Feeling a little more cheerful at seeing Gaskell discomfited, the inspector said, "Go fetch it then, and make sure you wrap it so that the fingerprints won't be rubbed off." Bertie de Grey, who had long since abstracted his mind from mundane proceedings, and had transported himself to rapturous curtain calls of the past, opened his eyes and said, "It won't matter, you know."

"What won't?"

"Finding the bottle and fussing about fingerprints. The gin in the bottle was not poisoned."

"Indeed. How do you know that, sir?"

"I saw Ally take a drink from it, and I assure you, Inspector, that he did not fall down and writhe."

"We have only your word for that, sir," said the inspector. He felt he was being made a fool of by this malign old man, and did not countermand his orders to Constable Gaskell, who came into the green room, looking sheepish and plainly wishing he had never mentioned the bottle of gin, since he now had to confess that he could not find it.

"Can't find it? Where did Mr. Jagat usually keep his gin, do you know, Mr. de Grey?"

"In the pocket of his mac, as a rule. Or in the drawer of his dressing table."

"We've been through his pockets and through the dressing room," Gaskell said. "In fact we've looked everywhere. There is no gin bottle."

"What kind of a bottle was it, Bertie," John Silk asked.

"Dear Johnnie, I thought you *knew*. What else have we been talking about? It was a bottle of *gin*."

"Yes, but what kind? Did you actually see it?"

"It was a pint of Bombay. Nasty stuff, I always think. Give me dear old Beefeaters any time."

A Happy English Child

It was plain from the look on Inspector Winterkill's face that if he could find a bottle of Beefeaters with some arsenic in it, it would be all up with Bertie de Grey. "Go ask Mrs. Barnes to come in a minute, Gaskell."

Mrs. Barnes came immediately, a small dry stick of a woman, as dried up and scrawny as her sister-in-law Lola Shrubsole was opulent. "Well, Harold," she said, reminding John Silk that Inspector Winterkill was a Rigby man. His first wife, from whom he was divorced, still lived in the town. The inspector had married a much younger woman; a girl, really. It had been a great scandal at the time. How like Rigby, John thought, to get all worked up over something as commonplace as a man leaving his dumpy wife of twenty years and going off with a young thing in a miniskirt.

"Hello, Mary," said the inspector. "How's Verity?"

"She's taking it very hard. If it's all the same to you, Harold, I'd appreciate it if you could wait till tomorrow to talk with her."

"Yes, of course. It's you I wanted to see, Mary. Did you do any cleaning backstage while the play was going on?"

"No, I never do. It isn't any use, is it." She glanced at the actors. "You only have to do it all over again afterwards anyhow."

"So you didn't empty any wastebaskets. Nothing like that?"

"I had a cup of tea with Lola and gave her a hand with the mending," said Mrs. Barnes, which her audience correctly interpreted to mean that Mrs. Barnes had mended and Lola Shrubsole had watched television.

"We're looking for Mr. Jagat's bottle of gin," said the inspector. "According to Mr. de Grey it was a pint of Bombay. If you come across it please don't touch it. Just let me know, or, if I'm not here, Troutt or Gaskell can take care of it. It's important."

"Of course," said Mrs. Barnes. "And now, if you don't

mind, Harold, I'd really like to take Verity home and put her to bed with a hot bottle. She's terribly upset."

"I think that would be quite all right," said the inspector. Ophelia, who had offered Verity and Mrs. Barnes a ride in her car, got up, and realizing suddenly that the missing gin bottle made suspects of all of them, sat down again.

John said, "I think if you have no reason for keeping her, Inspector, you might let Anne go, so she could take Mrs. Barnes and Verity in her car. I guarantee that no actor with an engagement that still has two months to run, is going to skip town, however guilty."

They all laughed at this. Gavin yawned again. "Sorry," he said. "I can't stop myself. Funny reaction, isn't it?"

"Quite a common one, really," said Inspector Winterkill. "I don't think we need keep you any longer. We can talk tomorrow," which polite formula Gavin correctly interpreted to mean, "It was you who poured the stuff down Jagat's throat, so don't leave town, will you."

"Does that permission to leave include the rest of us?" asked Bertie.

"Yes, Mr. de Grey. Everyone can go, for now."

"How very kind. Good night, my dears. Poor Johnny, how upsetting for you." He turned to the inspector and confided, "Ally has the ghastliest understudy."

After they had all left, Inspector Winterkill asked John to show him over the theater. They visited the dressing rooms, which were small, crowded and untidy. Barnes's carpentry shop was in an outbuilding next to the Theater Pub. It smelled appetizingly of sawdust and wood shavings. He kept it beautifully neat, but all the same, the inspector thought, it would take hours to sort through everything. Verity's prop room too was neatly kept, but full of unavoidable clutter; flower vases, cups, saucers and teapots were ranged on one shelf; swords, guns and pistols on another. Tables and chairs, ingeniously built by Barnes so that they could be folded flat, were stacked against a wall. Captain Hook's peg leg and skull and crossbones flag lay on a wall shelf, next to Yorick's skull, which wore, incongruously, an elaborate Edwardian lady's hat. If all of these rooms, tidily kept as they were, could provide hundreds of hiding places, Mrs. Shrubsole's domain, crowded, messy, with costumes jammed tightly together on racks, truly caused the inspector's heart to sink. If a bottle of gin was hidden here, it might take days to find it. As for a small bottle or a packet of paper which might have contained the poison, Inspector Winterkill doubted very much that they would ever turn up.

John, seeing his look of hopelessness, said, "Won't you come into my office. It's next to the boiler room and is the only place in this theater that's even moderately warm."

"It's the great drawback to Rigby," said the inspector, "being inland you don't get the view, but you still get the wind blowing off the North Sea."

John opened a drawer in his desk and brought out a bottle of whiskey. Inspector Winterkill, explaining that he was on duty, refused. He did so reluctantly. He would very much have liked a tot to cope with the disturbance in his gut caused by the take-away dinner from the Yellow Peril Restaurant his wife had brought home. The first Mrs. Winterkill would have walked down the street naked sooner than resort to take-away food, but greasy fish and chips, frozen fish fingers, Wimpies and Chinese take-away were Beryl's idea of cooking. Somehow, in the first flush of passion with a much younger woman he had failed to pay much attention to what he ate. Now it was too late. Discreetly he slipped a Rennie under his tongue while John poured himself a large whiskey, adding very little water. "I hope you don't mind if I have one," he said. "I confess I feel rather shaken. Poor Ally."

"Had you known him long?"

"Oh, dear me, yes. We toured the East together during the war, and we've worked together, on and off, ever since."

"Can you suggest any reason why anyone should want to poison him?"

"None," said John Silk without hesitation. "Ally was that rarest of creatures, an actor without an enemy in the world. He was a truly nice person, everyone liked him. I'm not just saying that in a *de mortuis* sort of way. It's true."

"What about Mr. de Grey?"

"Bertie? I don't suppose he cares for anyone very much. But that's not a reason to commit murder."

"Could it have been something political? Indians always seem to get so excited about politics."

"I really doubt it. He was Indian by birth, but he went to school here, and never went back to India at all. When we were there during the war I don't remember him ever looking up relatives. His parents were dead, I believe, and he was an only child. As far as I know he had no political interests at all. In fact, outside the theater I doubt that he had many interests."

"Boys?" asked the inspector, having picked up bits of gossip in the course of his interviews with the actors and theater staff.

John smiled. "Ah well, boys."

The inspector found himself wondering whether they were less troublesome than young women, but put the thought aside as irrelevant. He said, "Could you explain to me where everyone on stage was when the poisoning happened." He had looked quickly through the various depositions. Every actor had told the same story, which had aroused his suspicions, though it was hard to believe that all of them had conspired to poison a popular fellow actor. But they might be protecting someone.

"I can do better than that," said John Silk. "I can give you the papers on which I worked out the blocking." Seeing the inspector look blank, he explained that he was talking about the assigned places actors take during a scene. "It's none of it spontaneous, you know. When someone crosses the stage or sits down or gets up it's not the actor's inspiration, it's mine."

"Don't they ever feel inspired and move according to their own ideas?"

"They'd better not. Unexpected movements throw the other actors off. And of course never during fencing scenes. Every inch of swordplay is worked out in advance, otherwise it is simply too dangerous."

"And no one tonight moved differently from the way you blocked it?"

"Not until Claudius doubled over and fell on the floor."

"Did you watch it yourself?"

"Yes. I always do, not the whole play, of course, but a scene here or there, to keep the actors on their toes. I usually watch the fencing for the pleasure of it. Gavin Beauclerc, our Hamlet, is a lovely fencer. He fenced for the university when he was at Cambridge." John poured himself another drink, and without asking, poured one for the inspector, who pretended not to notice.

"What a name," he said. "Sounds like something out of King Arthur. Is it his own?"

"Yes, as a matter of fact it is. He wanted to change it to something more plebeian—Buckle, or Potts—it's funny, in Bertie de Grey's day actors all took very posh names, when I was young all the names, or at least most of them were very plain—Nell Wood, John Silk . . . I think we hoped if we kept them simple and short they'd go up in lights all the sooner. Now of course all the young actors want to sound as if they had been born in a Liverpool slum, so they can act in kitchen-sink dramas."

"John Silk's nice," said the inspector, taking an absent-minded drink and feeling it lap his stomach in soothing warmth. "Simple, but posh, if you see what I mean."

"My mother was Jenny Silk," said John, and seeing that the name meant nothing to the inspector, he said, "Before your time, I expect. She sang songs like 'The boy I love is up in the gallery . . . ,' danced a bit and showed a discreet ankle. She was very popular in her day."

"I often wish they'd go back to showing discreet ankles," said Inspector Winterkill, by which he meant he wished Beryl's miniskirts weren't quite so mini. "I don't hold with letting it all hang out, as they call it." He took a deep swallow from his drink. "Well, I don't see that there is any more to be done tonight. I'd better get back to Scarborough and write up my report."

If John thought that the acceptance of the drink he had poured for the inspector meant that he himself was off the hook as a suspect, he was to be disappointed. Though he knew himself to be innocent, there is something in the mere presence of the police which conjures up vague and undefined feelings of guilt. He was also very tired, and when the inspector took his leave it is possible that John wished him good night just a trifle too eagerly. The inspector, in whose stomach Chinese take-away, Rennies and whiskey were fighting a pitched battle, caught the note of relief and resented it. With the doorknob already in his hand, he turned back and said, "Troutt tells me you were the only one who was brave enough to drink the tea."

"Not brave, merely thirsty."

"I see. Of course there is one person who could have known with absolute certainty that the tea was not poisoned."

"The person who made the tea?"

"No. The poisoner."

John Silk decided that in spite of the unfortunate Nehru jacket and the too tight bell bottoms he was going to like Inspector Winterkill. "Ah," he said smiling, "that should make it all very easy for you."

CHAPTER II

On the morning after the murder John Silk breakfasted, as he did every morning of his life, on three small cups of China tea and two rounds of Melba toast, one of which it was his custom to leave untouched on the plate, simply to show his stomach who was in charge.

His night had been restless. Several times he had forced himself to waken from evil dreams, had told himself that it had all been a nightmare, only to remember that the horror had happened in fact, that poor, dear Ally was dead, murdered on the stage of the Rigby Rep, very likely by a member of the acting company. John, lying awake in the small hours, considered one by one the people who had been on stage with Algernon Jagat, and could not bring himself to believe any of them a murderer. Yet possibly, he thought, we are simply unable to imagine people we know as being capable of murder. Had Jack the Ripper been caught, was it not likely that all those who knew him longest and most intimately would have protested, "Not good old Jack. He couldn't hurt a fly."

Despite his restless night, John got up early and forced his body through the series of ballet exercises which had kept him limber since his earliest years in the theater. From the full-length mirror a rumpled morning face looked back at him, making him wonder, as he did every morning, whether it was time for another lift. From the back, he knew, his slim, straight figure and actor's ease of movement gave him the look of a still young man. But oh, that face.

"You should never have started," Ally had said only a day or two before, catching him at a make-up mirror. "I told you so at the time. Once you do, you have to do it again and again, or you'll end up looking like a basset hound."

Well, thought John, turning from these disagreeable imaginings, at least his teeth were mostly his own and he had kept his hair. Very fair in his youth, it was imperceptibly—to anyone but its owner—fading to white; an asset, he had discovered when, having fallen in love with a pretty Georgian house in the High Street, and determined to have it at any cost, he had done a series of lucrative television advertisements designed to convince Americans that if they drank a certain brand of sherry, or wore a particular kind of raincoat, they would instantly, and without effort, turn into English gentlemen.

The old woman who had owned the house before him had been confined to a wheelchair, and had fixed small mirrors to the drawing room windows so that, even housebound, she would miss nothing that happened in the High Street. John Silk, finding quite as much interest as she in Rigby's comings and goings, had never had them removed. It did not occur to him that his own windows, bare to the light of day, scandalized his neighbors, for Rigby did its spying decently concealed behind casement cloth and lace curtains.

His house stood at the exact point where the High Street curved, so that he had an excellent view of the goings-on at both the upper, fashionable end as well as of the lower part, which, disfigured during the war by a corporation dump, had made a number of very nice houses available to people who preferred a posh address to clean air. The Barneses, he knew, lived down there. He saw Mrs. Barnes now, returning from her morning's shopping, a basket packed with groceries in one hand, a bloody, dead rabbit dangling head down from the other. She did not, like the other shoppers, stop to talk (doubtless about the murder), but walked briskly along, merely nodding her head in greeting. Mrs. Barnes was a woman who kept herself to herself.

As John poured his second cup of tea he heard the newspaper flop through the slot in the door, and got up to fetch it. The murder had happened too late for the *Rigby Gazette* to do more than announce it in the stop press, promising a report from the medical examiner and an inquest. Unfortunately that would hardly prove to be the end of it. In a town so dull that its last major scandal—major by Rigby standards, not anyone else's—had happened nearly twenty years ago, when an alderman had got a Pierrot girl from Scarborough pier in trouble and had to resign his office, the murder of a well-known actor would be considered an absolute godsend by the local press. No doubt they would be hashing over every sordid detail for months to come. The Scarborough and Whitby papers would surely take a proprietary interest in the case, since the original Count Dracula had landed on the Whitby shore, and Ally's success in the part had been considerable.

John dreaded the publicity; the reporters and gapers and television cameras which were no doubt even now making their way toward Rigby. Certainly it would be good publicity—was there ever such a thing as bad publicity in the theater? No doubt they would be playing, for the rest of the summer season, to sold-out houses, with trippers from Scarborough and Whitby hoping to see another actor swallow rat poison and writhe on the floor. Death was good box office, but John felt only sadness at the prospect, as if a loved member of his family were being exposed to the curiosity and obscene speculations of the public.

Over his third cup of tea he planned his day. He would have to go down to the theater, to cope with the press and the police, but first he must go and notify his fellow members of the board of directors, Lady Biggle of Biggle's Breweries Ltd., and Sir Tancred Rievaulx, whose ancestor had built the theater for the amusement of the Prince Regent and his friends.

Knowing that Sir Tancred never got up till opening time, John decided to see Lady Biggle first.

Except for a languishing button factory, Biggle's Brewery was Rigby's main source of employment. For some years after the war, it too had languished, but a son-in-law's suggestion that they should introduce the distinctive peaty taste of Rigby's Golden Ale and Rigby's Velvet Stout to America, had proved a happy one. Lady Biggle had objected at the time that, once beer has been bottled and pasteurized for export, one kind tasted very like another, but the son-in-law, who had spent part of the war in Washington, assured her that Americans would buy almost anything so long as it was imported and they were allowed to pay a stiffish price for it. This had proved to be perfectly true. With a romantic label and a snobbish advertising campaign, Biggle's Golden Ale (the stout never really caught on) brought American dollars flowing in a gratifying stream into the long-suffering British economy and the Biggle bank account.

Lady Biggle did not live in one of the pretty Georgian houses which graced the High Street, but in a mansion placed high on the moor, built in a day when ostentation had it all over good taste, and more was definitely more. Ally had called it the Shatto, and had greatly rejoiced in its Palladian front, Victorian dovecote, Tudor stables, and a colonnade nearly as grand as Bernini's in Rome.

John climbed the steep hill along the bank of the river Rigg, which tumbled down brown and foamy, like good beer. At the top of the hill he paused to look back at the small town curving away from him, wondering, as he often did, that he, a Londoner, should have found such contentment here. When a mysterious bug, caught while making a film in India, had laid him low, and his doctor had advised a long rest, the offer of directing the Rigby Rep had seemed not only the next best thing to a rest, it had seemed the equivalent of being dead and buried. Since its heyday in the days of the Regency, when Rigby had been a flourishing spa, and gentry and the upper clergy had arrived with two full sets of clothes for before and after their cure, the little theater had declined, gently at first, but after the Great War precipitately, until it was hardly more than a useful hall for bingo and whist drives, with a shoddy pantomime at Christmas, and, in the summer, a creaky Maugham comedy, performed by over-the-hill actors for bored trippers.

Only the vigilance of the local Georgian society had kept the beautiful little theater from falling victim to a speculative builder. But with the arrival of the hush-hush genetic lab, and the prosperity of Biggle's Brewery, an interest in the theater revived, and John, having gently eased out the over-the-hill actors and bingo parties, had begun to build a solid repertory company, never quite of the first rank, but made up of reliable actors like Ally Jagat and Nell Wood, who had come very near to the top of their profession, and promising young ones like Gavin Beauclerc and Nigel Pratt, who were assuredly on their way up. Over the last few years London managers had begun to send scouts to the little Yorkshire town, as had the RSC, and young playwrights, finding the West End difficult to break in to, had begun to send their plays to John Silk. And, most notably, he had begun to involve a suspicious and reluctant town in the theater's activities. Saturday matinees for 'the kiddies' now vied with the local cinema, and the old age pensioners, who would go anywhere if there was free tea and buns, had their half-price performances, and discussion groups, of which Ethel and Enid Oakroyd were the leading stars. And John Silk, miles from his native and beloved London, had been happier here than he had ever been in his life. Now a murder had spoiled his bright accomplishment, whether temporarily or forever, he did not know.

The sky had clouded over as he had climbed the hill. A fine drizzle began to frost his coat and hair. He hurried up to the mansion. Lady Biggle had just finished breakfast, but offered to send for more for him. John thanked her and said he had already eaten. Lady Biggle had heard the news, of course, had indeed dismayed her daughter and son-in-law by bursting into tears on being told of the murder. She had been very fond of Ally, and now, speaking with John, began again to dab at her eyes. John was not surprised. He had often observed these friendships between stalwart old women and handsome men who do not compete with them on the field of virility. Ally had adored Lady Biggle in return, and she had been happily unaware that he found her, as well as her house, a tremendous joke.

"But who could have wanted to kill dear Algernon?" Lady Biggle asked. She was the only person who had always called him by his full name. On her tongue it assumed all the Edwardian grandeur his parents had probably hoped for.

They discussed this question at length but to no profit. "I wonder if it could have been someone Indian," Lady Biggle said. "They seem to be given to so much violence now that we are no longer there to keep order."

John was tempted to remind her that there had been occasional outbursts even in the days of the Raj, but knew it would have involved him in an even more time consuming and profitless discussion. "I don't think it likely," he said. "After all, he had lived in England since his schooldays."

"Dear Algernon, I shall miss his visits," said Lady Biggle. She mopped up a final tear and became practical. Tonight's performance would of course have to be cancelled, as a sign of respect as well as for practical reasons. It was to have been *The Importance of Being Earnest.* Ally as Lady Bracknell had shocked Rigby, but it had been a memorable performance, and John was saddened to think that he would never see it again. Since the police were in the possession of the body, no arrangements for a funeral could be made, but they decided to hold a memorial service in the theater the next afternoon. Lady Biggle pledged herself to provide food and drink for an informal get together afterward. "For," she said, "people are bound to talk, and they might as well do it between the four walls of the theater."

John thanked her and said he must find Sir Tancred to tell

him what arrangements had been made. Strictly speaking, he supposed, he should have gone to call on him first, since it was his ancestor who had built the theater and had contributed handsomely to its upkeep. Of all the Rievaulx wealth it was only the theater that had survived. The Hall stood roofless in untended woods, its grounds littered with cigarette wrappers and used condoms, while the last of the Rievaulx lived in lodgings, doing various unpaid county jobs. In his free time he could be found at the White Hart, kindly spending what little money he had to increase the revenues of Biggle's Breweries Ltd.

It was at the White Hart, therefore, that John bought two pints of Biggle's Golden Ale, which he took to the table where Sir Tancred sat behind an empty glass. Baby, his melancholy lurcher, sat under the table, her head on her master's knee. It was funny, thought John, how dogs came to look like their owners, or rather—much more likely—the owners came to look like their dogs. Baby, more greyhound than collie, had the same attenuated air, the same look of finding life just a bit too much to cope with, the same aura of faded khaki (hair, clothes, teeth, pelt all monochrome) as Sir Tancred. Both looked up with mild politeness when John asked permission to join them, but it was only Sir Tancred who thanked him for the beer. Baby, sniffing a steak and kidney pie John had remembered to buy, bided her time. She knew from long experience that her moment would come.

"Bad business," said Sir Tancred, when John asked him whether he had heard the news. "Who could possibly have done such a thing?" The pub had fallen oddly silent. John realized that they had been hashing this very question over when he had entered, and were too polite to go on in his presence. He unwrapped the meat pie and gave it to Baby, who swallowed it in two gulps, after which she returned to looking soulful. Sir Tancred's voice was nearly inaudible at the best of times. John, using an actor's technique, kept his audible only in the small corner where they were sitting. The pub, realizing that they would not glean any as yet undisclosed information directly from the horse's mouth, began to discuss the local rugby team.

"We simply don't know," said John. Well aware that pubs are breeding places for gossip, and quiet, steady drunks like Sir Tancred collect it about them as a branch in the river collects floating rubbish, said, "What's the village saying?"

Sir Tancred shrugged. "The usual, you know. Wogs, and pansies or whatever they call themselves nowadays, just asking for it . . . sorry, I expect you know the kind of thing."

John smiled, wondering when anyone had last used the word pansy.

"I shall miss Ally," Sir Tancred said. "He was a splendid drinking companion." John took the hint and signalled the barmaid for another round. "The thing about Ally," Sir Tancred went on, pretending not to notice that another beer was on its way, "is that he had discovered life's great secret —nothing Indian and transcendental, I don't mean that— just how to cope with boredom."

John Silk was much too busy running his theater to have to worry about boredom. He wondered how many drinks Sir Tancred had had already.

"You know what I mean," Sir Tancred said. "The boredom of great moments. Lovers transfixed by the moonlight. A suicide changing his mind at the sight of a butterfly's iridescent wing. How long they last, those moments! The butterfly may hover half an hour in the buddleia, the moon might be full all night, unless a merciful cloud hides it and we can decently yawn and go to bed. The nice thing about Ally was that he didn't bother. He knew that lad of his wasn't Phaedrus and wouldn't lead him to a celestial love. He liked the way his hair curled and his trim little bottom. I mean I ask you, what did Tristan and Isolde *do* all day? When Ally got bored with his little piece, he came to the pub and had a drink. Tristan couldn't do that, you see. No wonder he and

Isolde got so glum in the end. Yet Ally always got a tremendous kick out of the small things in life. I think he enjoyed himself nearly all the time. That's a very difficult thing to do. I hardly ever enjoy myself." He said this without self-pity, simply stating a fact. "I'll tell you what," he went on. "I went to see him at the Troutts' once. In the loo there was an empty gin bottle with two pieces of Queen Anne's lace stuck into it. Very pretty it looked too. I'd never thought about Queen Anne's lace one way or the other, it's just a weed after all. I knew Ally must have put it there. You can't think Mrs. Troutt did, or that young piece of his. And I thought how nice, every time he goes to have a pee he looks at those two flowers and gets a bit of a kick out of them. No rapture in front of a perfect rose. Just a little something to help you through another bloody day."

"Yes," said John, finding himself unexpectedly touched by Sir Tancred's boozy ramblings. "That sums up Ally very well. It's why he was such a pleasure to have around." He went on to tell him of his visit to Lady Biggle and the arrangements which had been made for a memorial service. On his way out of the pub he stopped at the bar and ordered another glass of ale for Sir Tancred. Mrs. Buxton, who was keeping bar, drew it for him and, determined to have something more than mere money from him, leaned her formidable bosom on the bar and said, "Dreadful about Mr. Jagat, isn't it. He was in here many a time. A very pleasant gentleman. Poison, they said it was. I was quite upset when I heard, Buxton will tell you the same. It really doesn't bear talking about."

"No, it doesn't," John said adroitly. "Thank you for being so understanding, Mrs. Buxton. I knew you would be," and before she could get into her stride to tell him how she had come all over faint, what she had said to Buxton, and what Buxton had said to her, he was out the door. "Londoners," she said indignantly to herself, the word Machiavellian not being in her vocabulary.

The murmur of talk rose even before John closed the door behind himself. He could not help smiling. Sir Tancred would be sure of free beers today, at any rate. Ally would have enjoyed the joke of that.

He walked back down the High Street, returning greetings, aware of the lingering looks, full of hope that he might stop and talk. The theater was down a side street, next to the assembly rooms, Rigby's major eyesore (not counting the button factory, the brewery and the council houses, which were hidden by the steep rise of Rigby Moor). Empty and derelict, its windows patched with cardboard and wood, its fountains full of rubbish, its baths rusted and dry, there remained in its perfection of proportion just enough hint of its former beauty to break the heart of a lover of Georgian architecture. This day however it was not the sight of the assembly rooms that caused John to sigh as he let himself into the back door of the theater, but a van belonging to Yorkshire Television, and an assortment of cars and bicycles belonging to the local press. A black car, easily recognized by its spit and polish as belonging to the police, was parked outside the main entrance of the theater.

CHAPTER III

Tim Selkirk awoke, wondering where he was and how he had got there. His tongue tasted like something forgotten in the cat's dish, his head seemed only precariously attached to his body, and ached so badly he wished it were not attached at all. When he at last succeeded in lifting his lids, which seemed to weigh a pound each, he discovered that he was lying fully dressed on top of the bed in the room Ally had rented from Mrs. Troutt. He still had no recollection of how he had got there.

Grade A peyote buttons my ass, he thought, remembering that bit at any rate. Either someone had sold Mick a pup, or else you had to be Carlos Castaneda to handle the stuff.

Cautiously he turned his head. He was alone in bed. Memory came in a rush. Ally, who had shared this pillow with him over the last few weeks, was dead. Oh Christ, poor Ally, poor bastard. His recollections were disjointed, as if he had watched events by the flicker of strobe lights.

It took him another moment before he remembered, among the fitful recollections of the evening, the word murder. Oh Christ! He sat up abruptly, causing his head to spin and to send a searing flash of pain through his sinuses. He paid no attention to the pain, but got to his feet and began tearing things from the closet and cupboards. Ally had been murdered, and at any moment the pigs would be here to search his room. How was it they had not arrived already? He looked at his watch. Six-thirty. Morning or evening? How long had he slept? He yanked back the curtain to find the sun barely risen and the sky a tender pink.

Oh shit, he thought, I got to sling my ass, let me get the

hell out of here before they get here. Frantically he turned his pockets inside out, collecting pills, a stash of hash, a plastic baggie filled with marijuana, too panicked to stop and swallow a Valium to lessen his anxiety. He bundled everything, pills, plastic bags, jeans and shirts into his backpack with only one thought, to get out of this room, out of town, back to London. He remembered that he had hidden some pills in one of the five pairs of Frye boots he owned, and began turning them upside down. The last boot, one of a new pair he had not broken in yet, held a small bag of Quaaludes and a roll of money he could not remember having put there. Indeed he could not remember having enough money lately to need to hold it together with a rubber band. Ally's, perhaps.

He took off the rubber band and began to count the notes. Seventy-five pounds. This must be the last of what Ally had left from the *Dracula* series, probably every penny Ally had owned in this world. With the bank notes there was a strip of white paper. Tim's head ached so badly he had difficulty focusing his eyes. Something was written on the paper. "For Tim," it said, "in case anything should happen to me."

His haste forgotten, Tim sat staring at the paper. Tears began to drop on it. His panic had left him as suddenly as it had gripped him; a chemical reaction from the peyote, probably, not a rational fear of the English police. He was not, after all, a suspect, he realized, or they would have arrested him last night. There was no reason for them to search the room, since Ally had been killed at the theater. If they wanted to go through Ally's possessions, they were welcome. All they would find would be a bottle of gin, a few books—of poetry, mostly—and his clothes.

He searched through his collection of pills, swallowed two Valiums, and rolled himself a joint. Slowly he began to feel better, though he still could not stop crying. Sniffling, he made himself a cup of tea on the gas ring, Ally's invariable remedy for a morning after. He wished he could stop thinking of him, of the small details of their life together. Why should he mind? They had been lovers but not in love. Ally had wanted a pretty boy to sleep with, and Tim had wanted a place to sleep. Hardly an arrangement to shed tears over.

He was so thirsty that he could not wait for the tea to cool, and burnt his mouth swallowing it. After a second cup he felt much better, but dreadfully tired. He went back to bed and fell at once asleep.

When he woke several hours later he felt perfectly restored, though still sad. Making certain that his landlady was not lurking on the landing, he took a towel and went to have a bath.

He fed a shilling to the geyser, and shaved while he waited for the water to get warm. Though English by birth, Tim had lived most of his life with his American mother after his parents' divorce, and could not get used to English plumbing. His bath, though scanty and tepid, made him feel much better. He went back to his room and dressed in a frilled and ruffled white shirt and tight bell bottoms. When he put on a pair of Frye boots he remembered the money and began to gather it up. Only now did the message on the note assume meaning. "For Tim, in case anything should happen to me." Anything? What had Ally expected to happen? A murder? If so, what am I supposed to do? Go to the police? No way.

For Tim the word police meant the visored ranks of Mayor Daly's pigs marching upon the peaceable flower children in Chicago's parks, for Tim's mind was capable of endless editing of events, until they suited the way he wanted to remember them. The scruffy, foulmouthed demonstrators in the park were confused in his memory with the smiling boys and girls placing sprigs of daffodils into the barrels of National Guard rifles, and he had completely forgotten that, whatever high-minded sentiments they had expressed for the television cameras, their motives had been far less admirable. As one of Tim's friends had put it the time: "I want to bring down the establishment and get laid. Mostly I just want to get laid."

Available drugs, and newly liberated women, who demonstrated their emancipation by never saying no, had briefly made of the peace movement a hedonist's paradise with background music by the Beatles. Such a life had made it hard to concentrate on scholastic subjects. When Tim discovered that he had failed every single one of his college courses due to lack of attendance, and had thereby lost his deferred draft status, he decided that the perilous life of a conscientious objector was not for him. The time had come to visit Daddy, otherwise known as Commander Selkirk, extra equerry to the Duke of Edinburgh. All this extra equerry business sounded like a drag and a downer, and Daddy was bound to be a stuffed shirt, but it beat going into the army. Tim charged airfare and a cash advance on one of his mother's many credit cards, and turned up on Daddy's Belgravia doorstep only to be told by a pained-looking stepmummy that his father no longer lived there. Daddy, it seemed, was not quite such a stuffed shirt after all, for his new address was a loft (or pad) in Covent Garden, which he shared with two smashing-looking birds called Arabella and Allegra. Their combined ages, Tim suspected, would not have added up to thirty-five. They were (or so they said) high-fashion models, and to prove it wore white lipstick and such heavy fake eyelashes that Tim could not imagine how they managed to keep their eyes open. Their miniskirts were the shortest he had ever seen, their slender legs the longest.

Daddy, returning from work at Buckingham Palace, expressed himself pleased to see his son in the mild Etonian manner so disconcerting to the more boisterous American spirit. He went to change his navy uniform for bell-bottom jeans and a cowboy shirt open to the navel, and settled himself on a tatami mat, where he began to roll joints of the best Acapulco Gold, straight from the diplomatic pouch.

Arabella and Allegra poured out wine into very large goblets, the joint was fantastic, and Tim felt he had died and gone to heaven.

He spent his days, while Daddy toiled at the palace, with Arabella and Allegra and the large group of their friends, and his evenings at clubs where rock groups he had never heard of played themselves into a frenzy and smashed their expensive electric guitars to smithereens, or else at the pad with people wandering vaguely in and out, drinking wine, smoking Acapulco Gold, and popping all kinds of interesting pills. Daddy did not in the least mind sharing his liquor, stash and women with Tim, nor did his son's presence at their various orgies cramp his style. It was Tim who began to feel queasy after a while. It is difficult for the rebellious young to live with a parent more hip than they are themselves. Tim was therefore not at all averse—when Ally, looking for a pretty boy to take to bed, caught his eye one night in an actors' pub—to transferring his person and five pairs of Frye boots from the loft in Covent Garden to Ally's picturesque and slovenly lodgings in a former firehouse in Fulham.

As far as sex was concerned, Tim honestly believed that he had no preferences. One of the very few books he had read while at Berkeley was Norman O. Brown's *Love's Body*, whose teaching he took to mean that everybody ought to go to bed with everybody else—regardless of gender—whenever the opportunity offered. He had practiced this simple creed for so long that he could no longer be sure what his preferences were. He had liked Ally, who was amusing company and fecklessly generous with money, but now, holding the note in his hand, reading for the seventh time the words: "For Tim, in case anything should happen to me," he very much wished he had never got mixed up with him. He was not usually plagued by an overly watchful conscience, but he did know that he owed it to Ally to take that note to the police. The thought that there was a murderer on the loose, someone who having struck at Ally might strike again, perhaps at Ally's pretty boy, weighed in on the side of conscience, while the memory of airfare and a cash advance charged against his mother's credit card, and the knowledge that she was quite capable of letting the police know about it, provided a counterweight. Still, it was often said in the papers how overworked the police were. They probably had better things to do than pursue so minor a crime, moreover one that had been committed across the Atlantic. All the same, Tim decided, he would keep away from the police station. He would take the note to John Silk, who could then turn it over to the police.

He gathered up his various pills and his marijuana in a plastic bag, which he hid behind the electric fire. He removed sixty-five of the seventy-five pounds in Ally's bundle, then wrapped two five-pound notes in Ally's message and put it in his pocket. It was nearly noon—his landlady would soon be home to prepare her son's dinner, and he decided to get out before she returned, for he knew she would ask questions. Not that she needed to. She was Constable Troutt's mother, and he had probably told her all there was to know, but she would undoubtedly wish to squeeze the last ounce of drama from the situation by talking with someone who had actually stood on stage at the moment Ally had died, and Tim was not in the right mood for this.

He did not know whether John Silk would be at home or at the theater, but had to pass his house in any case. His knock on the door was answered by Mrs. Pinn, the char, who said, "Afraid you've missed 'im, luv. 'E's down at the theater." She took a deep drag on the cigarette that dangled at the corner of her mouth. "You one of them actors, luv? It must 'ave been awful for you, seeing 'im die like that, right on stage, in front of every one. Mrs. Shrubsole says he took on something terrible."

Tim said yes indeed, and made off down the street, feeling that there had been little point in escaping Mrs. Troutt if he were to be trapped into a ghoulish conversation with Mrs. Pinn.

The heavy rain of the morning had stopped. There was a feathery mist in the air, which frosted his fair curls. The television crew and reporters were still standing under the awning of the assembly rooms. Earlier in the morning they had fanned out, talking to the villagers, getting a great deal of gossip and very little useful fact. The television crew had interviewed Lola Shrubsole, and still looked a little stunned. Everyone was cold and wet, longing for a drink and lunch. Several of them had indeed gone off to that fountainhead of gossip, the English pub, but while Inspector Winterkill's car was parked outside the theater, the rest remained with Casabianca-like devotion under the dripping awning.

Seeing Tim make for the actors' entrance, they converged on him, camera and pencils at the ready.

Tim loved being interviewed and filmed. During the Chicago riots, and a march on Washington—where with some of his more lunatic acquaintances he had unsuccessfully tried to levitate the Pentagon—he had been interviewed several times, but somehow he had always ended on the cutting room floor. No matter how unwashed and untidy he had tried to be, his fair curls and pretty face simply never looked scruffy enough for the cameras. But this time, he realized, he held a bit of information that would under no circumstances be scissored out by the editor. If he played this scene right, he might end up on the TV news all over England. Perhaps in America as well.

The reporters asked him whether he was an actor. Tim said he was, though aware that this was stretching things a bit. A damp, rather spotty girl who worked for the *Whitby Courant* said, "I thought you might be. You look like an actor. Were you in *Hamlet?*"

Tim said he was. Questions rushed at him, overlapping, never waiting for an answer. Had he been on stage when

Ally Jagat died? Did he know Jagat well? What kind of person had he been? Who would want to kill him?

Tim answered yes, yes and yes, he had known Ally very well indeed, was, as you might say, his protégé. They had shared lodgings at Mrs. Troutt's. He could see them drawing their own conclusions, but from previous experience familiar with the short attention span of the press, realized that he had forfeited their interest simply by mentioning another name, that in a moment they would be off to interview Mrs. Troutt.

"Look, please," he said, though no one was barring his way, "you'll have to excuse me. I have to see the inspector." It was a lie; he didn't want to see Inspector Winterkill in the least, but he reasoned correctly that the name would turn their interest from Mrs. Troutt back to him. He took the piece of paper from his pocket, looked at it and put it away again like one guarding a valuable secret.

Mrs. Troutt was forgotten. Had there been a new development? A suicide note, someone hazarded, while another ventured further afield to guess at some ancient Indian religious feud. Tim gave the television camera time to start turning and focus on him, then spread out the note with Ally's writing and the two five-pound notes. "I found it this morning inside one of my Fryes."

"Fries?"

"Boots. Frye boots."

"Oh, yes."

A hand reached for the note, someone asked whether he could tell them what it said. Tim took a step back and, remembering to talk directly to the camera, read it out. "For Tim, in case anything should happen to me."

It was sensational. Yorkshire Television and the Whitby and Scarborough papers had a scoop. As solicitously as if he were made of sugar and would melt in the rain, they drew Tim under the canopy of the assembly rooms. They put a microphone to his lips as if they were offering Holy Communion. Their questions came so fast that Tim could only answer one in five, but since they were all very nearly the same it did not matter. He told them that he did not know what the note meant, but that it sounded to him as if Ally—Mr. Jagat—had expected something to happen. Perhaps that was why he had split.

"Split?"

"Yes, split. You know, left London. Why else would a famous actor like Ally hide out in a Yorkshire village?"

Had Mr. Jagat ever mentioned any danger to him? No. Ally had never said that he feared for his life, unless you counted that note. No, Ally had never said anything. They grew bored with him again, he knew so little, they wanted to be off to get their news into print or on the air before anyone else heard it. The spotty girl from the *Whitby Courant* asked him whether he was American. He explained that he was English by birth, that his parents were divorced, that he had lived mostly with his American mother, that his father was Commander Selkirk, extra equerry to the Duke of Edinburgh. Usually any connection with royalty would have been followed up, but though they dutifully scribbled down the name, they were in a hurry now. Saying goodbye and thanks ever so, they mounted their bicycles or got into their cars and set off into the misty rain. Tim, feeling elated and deflated at the same time, looked after them, then shrugged and crossed the street to the theater, where Inspector Winterkill was drinking sherry with John Silk.

Tim was none too pleased to see him there, for he had hoped to use John Silk as an intermediary, so keeping a reasonable distance between himself and the police.

John introduced him, saying that he had been a close friend of Ally Jagat's.

"We've met," said the inspector, "though Mr. Selkirk may not remember."

"I don't," said Tim, smiling at him. He had a nice smile, and experience had taught him that people found it difficult to dislike him when he used it on them. "Like, I was wrecked. I don't even remember how I got home and to bed."

"You've Constable Troutt to thank for that," said John. "He very kindly offered to look after you."

"Yeah, I figured. I'm like really glad you're here, Inspector. I've been looking for you all over the place. I found this note this morning, and I knew you'd want to have it as soon as possible." He handed it over, together with the two five-pound notes.

"Is this what you were entertaining the press with?" asked Inspector Winterkill, entirely unaffected by Tim's charming smile. He handed the note to John, who read it and said, "Oh dear, I do wish you hadn't."

"Is it Jagat's handwriting?" the inspector asked.

"Short of being an expert forgery, yes, I would decidedly say it is. I probably still have his last letter to me in my desk at home, if you would like it for comparison."

"Thank you, that would be helpful."

Tim, feeling himself ignored, a child among grownups, said, "I thought it might be important. That's why I brought it right away. Do you think it means anything?"

As if he were indeed a child, the inspector ignored his question. Instead he asked, "Where did you find this?"

"Inside a pair of boots. I mean, inside one of a pair."

The inspector turned to John and said, "I'd better send Troutt to go over the room. I should have done it first thing, I suppose, but it was more important to search the theater." He turned to Tim. "Was the note exactly like this?"

Tim said, "Yes, with a rubber band wrapped around the two five-pound notes." He saw no reason to mention the other sixty-five pounds. They would do him more good than they would the police, and surrendering them would not bring Ally back to life.

"Do you have any idea what the note might refer to, Mr. Selkirk?"

"I guess it means he expected something to happen to him."

"Yes, naturally, but what? Mr. Silk says you were very close. Did he ever say anything to you that might shed light on the note? Did he mention any danger he might be in?"

Tim would have liked to dazzle the inspector with a piece of secret information, but had to confess that Ally had behaved just as usual; he had seemed neither nervous nor fearful, and John Silk, who had known Ally for many years, agreed that he had been his usual self. Yet there was the note, very likely genuine.

"It will have to be kept for evidence and fingerprints," said the inspector. He had not taken to the pretty boy in his dandified shirt and ragamuffin jeans, and he was well aware that the story of the note would be all over the paper and television by this afternoon, while he would have the press hanging around his neck, making his work three times more difficult than it need have been. If he could have afforded to indulge himself, he would have liked to plant a boot on the neat, denimed backside. "You'll be given a receipt," he said curtly. "And I'd strongly advise you, if you uncover any further interesting items in your boots or elsewhere, to come directly to the police instead of gabbling to the press. Goodbye, Silk. Thanks for the sherry. I'll keep in touch."

John, as keenly aware as the inspector that the press would make his life harder, would have liked to add a few unkind words, but reminded himself that Ally had been fond of the boy, and that despite his cocky airs and stupid behavior Tim was probably feeling lost and frightened, and offered him a drink instead. He did not suggest lunch, for though he felt sorry for the boy, he did not feel sorry enough to encumber himself for long with his presence. The young, while often pleasing to the eye, were, to John, simply too callow, too lacking in background and social polish, to be amusing companions.

They sipped sherry and talked a little. After Tim had

answered a few polite questions about his life in America and how he liked living in England, there seemed nothing left to say. "Well, goodbye, I'm busy," seemed to John a little harsh, so he said, "If you ever feel you want a talk, please do feel free to come and see me." It amused him that Tim looked shocked at what was surely the mildest and least sincere of invitations. "That was *not* meant as a pass," he added, hardly able to keep from laughing.

"I don't mind passes," said Tim, true to his code of never saying no to a proposition.

"I thought you looked a little shocked," said John, "rather as Gertrude might have when Claudius proposed to her over the funeral baked meats."

Tim, who had no idea what John Silk was talking about, said, "It's just that you sounded so much like Ally there for a minute. It was the kind of thing he used to say."

"It's the kind of thing that comes naturally to people of Ally's and my generation. A polite formula, nearly meaningless."

"Then why say it if you don't mean it."

"It's a form of civility."

"Sounds more like hypocrisy to me."

"No, decidedly not hypocrisy. Hypocrisy cheats. Civility merely serves to round off the harsher edges of life."

"Who needs that?"

"All of us. Every beastliness from mayhem on the motorway to nuclear war is caused by lack of civility."

Remembering the notable lack of it between the protesting students in Chicago and Mayor Daly's police, Tim said, "Maybe you've got a point."

"Certainly. Just think, if heads of state were to say, 'Please have another slice of my colonies,' as a hostess does with the roast beef, and they all said 'After you, old chap' at the door instead of pushing and shoving to have the biggest and nastiest bombs, no one would ever manage to get a war going."

"Unless your dinner guest is a hog who takes all the roast beef and tramples everybody at the door."

"Exactly my point," said John. "That is why civility is so important."

CHAPTER IV

The morning had not gone particularly well for Detective Inspector Harold Winterkill. The business of the murder had kept him up very late the night before, and his alarm clock had awakened him almost as soon (he felt) as he had fallen asleep. Gritty-eyed and empty of all but yawns he entered the police station and headed directly for the large tea urn. The tea was black and thick and seemed to snarl at him as it poured into the cup. Aware that it had sat there stewing all night and would do his stomach no good, he added a generous amount of condensed milk, changing the brew's color from black to dark gray, like a sky before a storm. The amused look on the face of Constable Maggie Stein at the desk was something he could well have done without. It reminded him of the time when she had first joined the police. He had very politely asked her to make a fresh pot of tea, and had been told crisply that the possession of a penis did not, as far as Constable Stein could see, disable him from making his own tea. Since then he had treated her with the same caution he would have accorded a ticking parcel with an Irish postmark.

There was a plate of stale buns stuck full of what looked like black beetles, but were really only scorched sultanas. He munched one of these, washing it down with the charcoal gray tea. Mavis, the first Mrs. Winterkill, had always had a hot breakfast for him, no matter how early he had to be at work. She'd held his coat and umbrella for him, and afterward had stood in the window, surrounded by flowering plants, to wave goodbye. Of course you couldn't expect that kind of thing from Beryl, who slept till the last possible moment, and did her nails, hair and elaborate make-up at the hairdresser's where she worked.

However, thought the inspector, Mavis had weighed eleven stone and had slept with curlers in her hair, and she had never, never, as he had kissed her goodbye of a morning, whispered in his ear, "Time for a quickie, luv," as Beryl often did. And you had to hand it to Beryl. She might not be able to cook or keep house or get up in the morning to make breakfast, but her quickies were memorable. This morning, however, she had simply turned away, yawning and mumbling, "You off then, luv?" and had gone back to sleep.

"Well, I must hie me to Rigby," said the inspector.

"Oh, they've given you the Jagat case, have they?" Constable Stein's tone of voice implied that this was a bit of luck for the murderer. As if Inspector Piggot, a dozy chap if ever there was, could have caught anyone. Still, Inspector Winterkill was not at all sure of his own powers in unravelling a case in which a lot of people could have done the murder, someone had done it in full sight of a theater audience, there was no apparent motive, and no known enemy. The obvious suspect, Tim Selkirk, the young man with whom Jagat had been living, had by all reports been in no condition even to swat a fly. The ambulance crew, who were all too familiar with the symptoms from their attendance at rock concerts, had assured the inspector that the young man was, as they put it, definitely wrecked. And if the poisoned gin had been in the bottle, the field widened to include everybody from Rigby and surrounding territory.

The inspector sighed. All he could do was to slog through the usual procedures—check the background of the dead man (he was after all an Indian, and Indians, as everyone knew, were an excitable lot who couldn't even hold an election without massacring a few thousand of their fellow citizens) and, boring as it was, interviewing every single subscriber who had attended the performance. It was not a prospect to put a sparkle in a detective inspector's eye.

At the Rigby police station, remembering Gaskell's officiousness the night before, he gave himself the pleasure of assigning that eager young constable to the corporation dump to supervise the search through Rigby's rubbish for the missing bottle of gin. He asked Troutt whether he had heard any gossip that might be of interest. Not really, said that constable, except that Mrs. Barnes and Nell Wood, the actress who played Queen Gertrude, had had a rare old dust-up.

"Oh, really," said the inspector, brightening up. "At the theater, was it?"

No, it had been at Mrs. Barnes's house, and loud enough for a neighbor who was pegging out her washing to hear every word.

"When did this take place?"

"Oh, three, four weeks ago."

Grumpily, the inspector said that this was hardly helpful information, seeing that it had happened some time back, and neither lady happened to have been poisoned.

Constable Troutt, aware that he had annoyed the inspector, offered to interview any locals who had been at the theater, and Inspector Winterkill accepted with relief. Ever since his divorce from Mavis and his marriage to Beryl, the ladies of Rigby had regarded him as an ardent trade-union member might regard a blackleg, and though nothing was ever said to his face, their speaking silence conveyed very plainly what they thought of him.

"Thanks Troutt, that will be a help. I'm going down to the theater, to see how the search there is coming along. Not that I expect them to find anything, poor sods. Oh, by the way, leave Mary Barnes to me. There's something I want to ask her." It probably had nothing to do with the case, but it did seem odd, and anything odd had to be checked in a murder investigation. Why had Nell Wood gone to Mrs. Barnes's house when she could see her any day at the theater?

A Happy English Child

Inspector Winterkill, who was a considerate man, planned to interview the actors in the afternoon, assuming that theatricals habitually slept late. However, as he passed the house where Nell Wood lodged, Mrs. Bridges, the landlady, was shaking a rug out the window, and on being asked said, dear her, Miss Wood had been up for some time. Giving the rug a final shake directly over the inspector's head to show him what she thought of a man who divorced a wife of twenty years to marry a young chit who was probably no better than she should be, she offered to ask Miss Wood whether she could see the inspector. In a moment she stuck her head out the window again and said the door was on the latch and the inspector was to go straight up, first door on the left.

Nell Wood had the best room in the house. Its windows faced the High Street, and the bath was directly across the landing. Judging by its neatness—the bed already made up, a fire laid ready, though not lit—the inspector guessed that Nell Wood kept her landlady to a standard with which Mrs. Bridges, known for slatternly ways, had until then been unacquainted.

Nell had just finished a meal which might have been either a late breakfast or an early lunch. A small table by the window was set with an embroidered cloth. The teapot, cup and saucer, plate, sugar basin and milk jug were all of a matching pattern, and a very pretty one, too. The remains of a boiled egg rested in a flowered egg cup; the jam was served in a bowl which matched the cup. The silver looked, to the experienced eye of the policeman, to be both old and of excellent quality. Most certainly it had not come from Mrs. Bridges's kitchen.

"Good morning, Inspector," said Nell, getting up to greet him. "Will you have a cup of tea? I'm a fairly late sleeper, we all are when we're not doing films, so I always have a kind of breakfast-*cum*-lunch. I believe Americans call it brunch—a dreadful expression."

Inspector Winterkill accepted a cup of tea. "I didn't know Mrs. Bridges was so indulgent with lodgers," he said. "I should have thought breakfast from eight to nine, egg and ham, or sausage and tomato would have been more her style."

"Oh, Bridges has nothing to do with it except for a pot of hot water. I do my own washing up in the lav. I wouldn't dream of letting Mrs. Bridges touch my few remaining bits of the family Lowestoft."

"I thought it might be," said the inspector. "I was in on an investigation of stolen china once—it was Staffordshire, not Lowestoft, but I learned a bit about the subject."

"The travelling life hasn't done it much good," said Nell, pouring herself a cup of tea and adding a drop of milk. "I wish I could be casual about such things, like the young; eat with my fingers from a paper plate. It saves such a lot of bother, doesn't it? But there it is. I was brought up in a family where one always ate egg with a silver spoon, and nothing was ever put on the table in the container in which it was bought. All of which presupposes a drudge somewhere behind the scenes, ready to polish tarnished silver spoons and do huge washings up. Now that the days of cheap servants are no more, I find I keep right on doing these absurd things, even though I am now the drudge."

"I like to see standards kept up," said the inspector, thinking of the paper cartons from the Yellow Peril take-away.

"Will you have some more tea, inspector? I wish I could offer you a drink, but I don't dare keep it in the house. It's the ultimate test for recovering alcoholics, you know, to be able to keep a bottle for one's friends and guests, but I haven't arrived at that state of serenity yet."

"That's all right, I don't want a drink," said the inspector, not quite truthfully. "What I really want is to talk with you about last night. You were on stage when it happened, and I wonder whether anything might have struck you as out of the ordinary. I know I asked you that yesterday, but I think everyone was in a state of shock, and I wonder if anything might have come back to you since then."

"I think I'm still in a state of shock," said Nell. "I simply can't take it in. I have to keep reminding myself that Ally is dead. I can't convince myself that it really happened, and that I watched it happen."

"It's always like that with a sudden death. I was told that at the previous performance of *Hamlet* someone put gin into your goblet."

"I expect it was meant for a joke."

"It seems a cruel joke. It might have made you go back to drinking again, mightn't it?"

"Yes, quite easily. But I didn't swallow it. It's odd, you know, just the smallest taste and I found myself spitting. Well, not spitting, exactly—I expect it was the surprise, really. Like people who've given up smoking and choke on a cigarette when they try to take it up again."

"Do you have any suspicion at all of who might have spiked your drink?"

"No. Most people at the theater know that I'm working very hard at keeping off the stuff, and I really don't think anyone tried to get me drunk. I think it was a simple mistake. The goblets got mixed up, that's all."

"Would you say Jagat was a drunk—sorry—an alcoholic?"

Nell thought this over. The inspector, misinterpreting her silence, said, "Do you mind talking about the subject? We needn't, if you'd rather not."

"Not a bit. In AA they positively encourage one to talk about it. It's what makes so many ex-alcoholics such bores. I don't know about Ally. Borderline, perhaps. He had such lovely manners, he never appeared to be drunk, and he didn't drink when he was working, but he did put away rather a lot and I doubt that he could have got through the day without it."

"And Mr. de Grey?"

"Poor Bertie. I shouldn't think there's any doubt about him at all."

"There seems to be an awful lot of drink about somehow. Jagat and his gin, de Grey, someone spiking your drink . . ."

"There's a lot of alcohol about everywhere. If someone had poisoned Ally's tea you'd suddenly notice that there was a lot of that about."

"Yes, probably." The inspector got up and took his leave. Half out the door he turned back and said, "Oh, by the way, is it true that you had some trouble with Mrs. Barnes?" He thought she looked startled, but perhaps it was only at his sudden introduction of a new subject. In any case she recovered her poise so quickly that he could not be sure he had not imagined it.

"Mrs. Barnes?" said Nell. "I don't see very much of her. Her job doesn't start till the play's over and we are going home."

"I see. I thought there was a story about a quarrel, that you went to see her at home and there was some unpleasantness."

Nell began to laugh. "Oh, dear, yes. But that was ages ago. I didn't go to see her. It was Barnes I went to see. I wanted him to do a repair for me—a wooden box I used the first time I did Portia. The cast gave it to me as a present when I left. I've been using it as a jewelry box since then, and when a corner broke off I thought Barnes might be able to mend it for me. He's a very good carpenter. Unfortunately Mrs. Barnes mistook my motives, if you can believe it."

The inspector could not help smiling. Barnes, that timid little mouse of a man, was hardly the answer to a maiden's prayer, though it seemed rather touching that Mrs. Barnes, after a good many years of marriage, should still regard him as such.

"What made you go to the house?" he asked. "Barnes is usually at the theater, isn't he?"

Nell poured herself another cup of tea. With a small frown she said, "What does all of that have to do with Ally's murder, Inspector?"

"Sorry. I'm all too apt to go off on tangents, the super always tells me."

"To tell you the truth, I wanted to see what she'd done with that lovely house. Plastic covers on the furniture, I expect, and a dish of plastic fruit on the telly."

"Very likely," said the inspector, thinking, bloody, snobby bitch. "Everyone in town has that bowl of plastic fruit. It's the first prize at whist drives. My former wife had one. Well, Miss Wood, you've been very patient putting up with me. If you remember anything else, you will let me know, won't you."

"Of course, Inspector."

As he opened the door his attention was caught by a framed calendar reproduction depicting a madonna holding a fat, uncircumcised baby. Popery in any of its aspects being repellent to a good Rigbyite, the inspector turned away as if he had witnessed an obscenity. Nell laughed and said, "It's pretty awful, isn't it. But it's Mrs. Bridge's pride and joy. I daren't take it down. Anyhow, the colors are the reproduction's fault, not Raphael's. It's a lovely painting, really. Do you have children, Inspector?"

"No, we never had any. I can't say I regret it. As a policeman you soon learn that they are more trouble than they are worth."

"Oh, but surely that isn't true in every case. Look at Verity Barnes. Surely she's never been a moment's trouble to her parents."

"I don't suppose she has. Verity is a nice girl. But she's in the minority these days, I can assure you."

"I expect she always would have been. The young are just more open about things nowadays."

It suddenly occurred to him that Beryl was only a few years older than Verity. "I dare say you're right," he agreed.

"I can't say it's an improvement. It wouldn't hurt them to practice a bit of decent hypocrisy now and then."

It was close to tea time before the inspector found himself at the bottom of the High Street. He had finished interviewing the actors and most of the theater staff without result, and was both hungry and thirsty. When Mrs. Barnes opened the door to him, a smell of homemade eccles cakes assaulted him with such force that he began to salivate like one of Dr. Pavlov's dogs. Mrs. Barnes showed him into the best room, which was furnished in pale blue silk. Nell Wood had been wrong about the plastic slip covers, he noted with some satisfaction. Mary Barnes would never resort to such compromise. A fanatically proud housekeeper, she would keep the pale blue furniture as slickly shining and spotless as the day she had bought it, by the simple expedient of never allowing anyone to use it.

Harold Winterkill, who had after all grown up in Rigby, realized that being shown into this room was not an honor, but a rebuke. It served to tell him that he was no longer regarded as one of them—that by divorcing Mavis and marrying a girl with long blond hair and long slender legs, he had forfeited membership in the tribe and had become an outsider. Had he still been one of them, he would no doubt have been shown into the room the family used every day; a room far pokier than this one, crammed full of comfortable, overstuffed furniture grouped around the telly, no doubt decorated by Nell Wood's despised bowl of plastic fruit.

Mrs. Barnes excused herself to take the cakes from the oven. The inspector, tormented by the delicious smells of baking, wondered whether she would ask him to tea. He knew how deeply she disapproved of him—middle-aged women were a bleeding trade union; divorce one and you divorce them all—but all the same he hoped he would be offered a cup of tea and a piece of home-baked cake. It surprised him that she had a proper tea on a week day—he would have thought high tea or an early supper would be more in her line—but when she stopped in the doorway, a tray held in front of her, and said, "I'll just take Verity her tea if you'll excuse me, Harold. You'll stay and have a cup," he realized that the tea, the lace covered tray, the rose in its bud vase, were all done for her daughter, for whom no fuss was ever too much, no trouble too great.

"How is Verity?" he asked.

"She's upset. I've kept her in bed for the day. I hope it's not her you've come to see, Harold. I've only just got her so she agreed to have a drop of tea and a bite to eat."

"I do have to see her," the inspector said. "But it'll be only for a moment, and I promise I won't upset her."

Mrs. Barnes was gone a long time. Bored by the chilly, neat room, the inspector went to the window and pushed aside the curtain. The best room faced out the back; in fact, it looked directly out on the corporation dump. But this was not the sight that met Inspector Winterkill. He saw instead a vegetable garden, its rows spaced evenly and planted so straight they reminded him of soldiers on parade. Scarlet runners climbing up tall poles blocked the view of the dump, and behind them a hedge of sweet peas, trained neatly up a trellis, made a second screen if the first should fail. Both sides of the garden were bordered by roses, all of which seemed to be in bloom. Not one was faded, there was not a leaf yellow with blackspot to be seen. Had it not been for the gulls wheeling and screaming in the sky, there would have been no sign that the house was next to a rubbish tip.

"That's Barnes's garden," said Mary, who had come in without his noticing. Her tone had that dismissive note wives use when they speak of husbands building ships inside bottles or collecting stamps, activities of no earthly use but tolerated because they kept the menfolk home and out of trouble. She laid the table with a lace cloth, the good china tea pot and a Wedgewood cake plate piled with a pyramid of cakes. She might not approve of her guest, but having invited him, everything would be done perfectly.

After she had poured out the tea, the inspector said, "I suppose you realize I'm here on business, Mary. You and Verity were almost the last people who saw Jagat before he went out on the stage. Can you tell me exactly what was going on backstage just before that?"

Mrs. Barnes took a sip of tea and thought a while. When she spoke, the inspector knew, her answer would be clear and truthful. Mary Barnes was not one to go off in all directions, the way most women did.

"You know about the light going out," she said. "We all stood in the dark, except for matches or cigarette lighters. I think someone jostled the table with the drinks on it, because Verity said 'Oh please be careful,' or something like that. Barnes fixed the lights, and I helped Verity carry the table on the stage. She said something about making sure Mr. Jagat's goblet was on the right, and took a sniff to be quite certain. Then we left the stage. I went back to finish my tea with Lola, but Verity stayed to watch. She was a bit gone on Mr. Jagat, ever since she saw *Dracula* on the telly."

It surprised the inspector that Mrs. Barnes took this so calmly, but she had probably realized that in the case of Jagat she had very little to worry about.

"Is that why she is so upset?"

"That, and seeing it happen. Verity can't bear the sight of anything dead. It's always Barnes or I have to take the dead mice from the trap."

"I suppose mice are a problem down here so near the tip," said the inspector.

"They're not so bad now Barnes got the terrier. She's a wonderful ratter, much better than a cat, and she doesn't shed so much either. I go over her with the Hoover once a day and you hardly know there's a dog in the house."

"Has Verity spoken to you about it at all?" the inspector asked. "Did she say anything about what she saw."

"No. I can't mention the subject or she goes off crying. It's best to let her forget."

"I'll have to see her, Mary. I'm sorry."

"Yes, of course, I understand that. You have to do your job, same as anybody. But try not to upset her."

Mrs. Barnes got up and led the way up the stairs. When she opened the door to Verity's bedroom, the inspector saw over her shoulder that Verity slid something quickly under her pillow. Her tea tray seemed scarcely to have been touched, and Verity, red and blubbery with crying, offered him a shaky hello. Mrs. Barnes collected the tray and went away. The inspector looked around Verity's room, which was like something out of a fairy tale, all lace and dimity and ruffles. A canary cage hung by the window. Its occupant was making his confident way through a tricky coloratura passage, and paid no attention to the visitor.

The inspector apologized for bothering Verity, who said it was quite all right, she was sorry to be such a silly, but every time somebody spoke nicely to her it seemed to set her off crying again.

"Perhaps I'd better bark at you," he suggested, and earned a watery smile. Her story was just like her mother's. She didn't know, she said, who had jostled the table, they'd all been crowded together and it might have been anyone. She'd never heard any gossip around the theater that might have indicated that Ally Jagat had an enemy, on the contrary, he was very much liked by everyone. "Even Lola Shrubsole?" the inspector asked. Oh well, Mrs. Shrubsole didn't like foreigners, Verity admitted, but that was no reason to kill them. Inspector Winterkill agreed regretfully. "I won't trouble you any more today, Verity," he said. "Just one more thing? What have you hidden under your pillow?"

Verity blushed. "Come on," said the inspector, "I saw you hide something."

Still rosy with blushing, she brought out the Cecil Beaton photograph.

"I should look round for a younger chap," said the inspector. "And try to stop crying, and eat your supper, won't you. It's worrying your mother, you know."

Verity nodded. "I know. I'll try, truly."

"It's a very pretty room," the inspector told her, looking around. The canary hit a high C and almost fell off his perch. Verity laughed. "There, that's better," said the inspector. "Goodbye, Verity."

Mrs. Barnes was waiting for him downstairs. He assured her that Verity was fine, and took his leave. At the door he remembered that he had one more question. "What was the dust-up you had with Miss Wood, Mary? I'm told they heard you two all the way to the button factory."

Mrs. Barnes looked disgusted. "Her, you mean. I hope I never raised my voice like a fishwife. That woman, can you imagine it, coming here creeping around after Barnes. They do say she can't keep her hands off anything in trousers, but as I told her, Barnes was spoken for, trousers or not."

"What did Barnes have to say to it all?"

"I didn't trouble myself to tell him."

"Quite right, he might get a swelled head. Well, thank you Mary, for the delicious tea. Those cakes were the best ever."

"I don't suppose you get much home baking these days," she said, rubbing it in.

"There's other things than food in the world," said the inspector, but he did not sound entirely convinced.

In her room, Verity Barnes put her hand under the pillow and brought out, not the Cecil Beaton photograph, but a torn corner of cheap writing paper. Its edges were scorched, as if someone had begun to burn it, but had changed his mind. Words cut from a newspaper were glued to the writing paper. The first line, with the 'l' nearly scorched away, said EAVE US BE. Underneath this was another part of a line. It said: TIME WILL BE with a word that might be IT so badly scorched that she could only guess.

Verity held this scrap of paper and looked at it for a long time. Then she began to cry again. In spite of her promise to the inspector, and a sincere wish not to upset her parents, she decided not to come down for supper. When next her mother looked in on her, she pretended to be asleep.

Constable Gaskell's day at the corporation dump was not only unappetizing, but frightening and humiliating. He was terrified of rats, for one thing, and he found the men working the rubbish tip a disconcerting group—an army of dusty and predatory mercenaries who regarded the dump as their kingdom and seemed to be amused by his uneasy presence. While sorting with knowledgeable speed through each lot of rubbish as it arrived, putting aside anything that might be of further use or could be resold, they took it in turns to ignore and patronize the constable.

" 'S not much good here," a very large dustman told him. "Liverpool's a place you can turn a nice penny. There's nothing people in big cities won't throw away. Now the locals here," he said, with the contempt of a city man for the provinces, "they're a tight lot. If they honest to Gawd can't use something any more, they wrap it up and give it as a wedding present."

"You're supposed to be looking for a bottle of Bombay gin," said the constable, in an ill-judged attempt to establish his authority. Standing in a cold wind blowing off the Dales, with gulls screaming in frustration above his head, did little for his self-esteem. But snubbing the large man from Liverpool did even less.

"Ar," said the dustman, with the patronizing kindness of a grizzled veteran showing a frightened young lieutenant over the trenches. "The locals drink beer, mostly, so a bottle of gin won't be 'ard to find, if it's 'ere, of course."

The men ate their midday meal right at the tip, amid the smells of decaying rubbish and smoldering ash. Constable Gaskell had not thought to bring a lunch. When they kindly offered to share their pies and sandwiches (stuffed with slices of bleeding beef) he was so cold and miserable that he did not have the backbone to refuse their offer. But as he ate he was conscious of the angry gulls, and imagined the eyes of millions of ravenous rats fixed on the food in his hand.

He had always been terrified of rats; memories of *1984* and the stories an uncle had told him about the rat-infested trenches of World War I kept going through his head. "We put a terrier down a trench one time," his uncle had told him. "We thought he'd make a good job of the rats. But in the morning there was nothing there; not a bleeding thing. Well, no, I'm telling a lie. There was a bit of bloody terrier fur. That's how we knew he hadn't just run off, the poor little blighter."

Constable Gaskell wished he hadn't remembered that story. His eyes moved amid the tins and paper bags until one of the workers, his great belly hanging out of the waist of his trousers like a challenge, said, "Don't worry about the rats, lad. They don't come out till sunset. Of course once it gets dark the place is alive with them. That's why the gulls are carrying on so. They want us out of here so they can have a feed before the rats take over."

Gaskell thought he might do the gulls a favor and clear out in time for an early tea. Surely by four he could leave without losing face. When the minute hand on his watch touched the top he breathed so great a sigh of relief that the ashes at his feet stirred in a brief dance. He said goodbye to the rubbish men, who were loading their lorry with the objects they had scavenged, and was almost out of earshot when he thought he heard his name called. Perhaps he had only imagined it. Or a malevolent wind whistling over the Dales had made it sound like, "Hoy, you there!" Yes, that must be it. He walked on, trying to persuade himself of the truth of this. But the man who was calling him had a chest like a beer barrel and a voice that could have been heard across a battlefield. " 'Ere, Copper, come and have a look at this," he shouted, and even poor Gaskell could not attribute so long a sentence to the wind. There was nothing for it. He had to turn back.

"Yes, what is it?" he said, impatience unconcealed in his voice.

The large man held out a scrap of paper. "Dunno if it's anythink," he said. "Might be."

Gaskell looked down at a corner of writing paper, the cheap kind found at every Woolworth's. Its edges were ragged and scorched. Words cut from a newspaper were glued to the stationery. Gaskell found an envelope in his pocket and asked the dustman to drop the scrap of paper into it.

"Lucky you were wearing gloves," he said, unable to bring himself to show gratitude. "You'll be sure not to touch anything you think might be of interest to the police, won't you? Any more bits of this paper, and of course the bottle. Oh, if there should be anything in it, don't drink it, please. It might just be poisoned."

The dustman, looking amused, touched his cap and said, "Right you are, guv'nor." As he walked away, Gaskell heard him say something to his companions, followed by laughter. He had a nasty suspicion that they were laughing at him.

At the police station he carefully put the scorched piece of Woolworth writing paper on a piece of clean blotting paper. It looked as if it had spent some time in the rain, and newsprint being what it was these days, the words were smudged. But they were not difficult to read, though, comprising only one fourth of the letter, they made no sense. AS ONLY A WAR, the top line said, and the second one—what there was of it—read: UT AND LEA. AS ONLY A WAR might be considered to have some meaning. "As only a war can be," perhaps. UT and LEA was like something from a Scrabble game. UT might be hut, shut, cut, out; LEA could be leave, leaf, lead, leach, leap—dismayed at the readiness with which words starting with "lea" were coming to mind, Gaskell decided to leave it to Inspector Winterkill, who had just entered the police station. At least, failing the bottle of gin, he had not returned entirely empty-handed.

"A poison-pen letter, obviously," he said in the superior manner which so annoyed his betters, and would cause him to draw rubbish tip duty for another day. "You can see the threat. Something to do with war. The rest might have been 'get out and leave.' I don't think we'll have much luck with fingerprints. It seems to have spent some time out in the rain."

Inspector Winterkill looked amused. "Very ingenious, Gaskell," he said. "You may even be right. Perhaps someone was declaring war, though that doesn't help us to know on whom."

Constable Gaskell, at all times ready to enlighten his elders, said, "Obviously on Jagat. The paper wasn't with the theater rubbish, but it was very windy today, it might have been blown about."

"Someone declaring war on Algernon Jagat. He reads it, tries to burn it, changes his mind, tears it up and throws it away. And the next thing he knows he's dead. Yes, it's a lovely theory. The only trouble is, while you're out there looking for the gin bottle tomorrow, you may find piles more of these. Didn't you see the program on the telly Saturday night? *Death by Mail,* I think it was called. All about a young lad who sets a whole village by the ears sending out poison-pen letters. And that's how he did it, with words cut from a newspaper and glued to a page of stationery. Sneating was livid when he came to work yesterday. Seems his nipper cut the whole Sunday paper to shreds before he could settle down to it, playing poison pen. Yes, I expect you'll get a lot more of these. It was a rainy Sunday, if you'll remember. I can picture many a mother keeping her kids quiet with the newspapers, a pair of scissors and some glue. But while you're out at the tip tomorrow, do please try to remember that what you are looking for is a bottle of Bombay gin."

It was close to supper time when the inspector finished his business at the police station. Mrs. Barnes's eccles cakes, rich though they had been, had worn off, and he felt renewed pangs of hunger. He should be on his way home to Beryl, but tea with Mary Barnes had put him in mind of better things. What he wanted was a solid, home-cooked dinner, the kind Mavis had had waiting for him every night; roast beef and Yorkshire pudding, or a nice rabbit pie with a crust that melted in your mouth. He might call round and see how she was doing. They had parted without hard feelings, so far as he knew. He had let her keep the house and paid her a handsome alimony every month. Beryl thought he ought to stop now that Mavis had a job at the button factory, but, as he tried to explain to her, you don't put aside a woman who's cooked and scrubbed for you for twenty years without some compensation. It wouldn't be fair. Even Maggie Stein, he thought, would have approved of this noble sentiment.

He caught Mavis on the doorstep, where she was trying to hang on to several bags from the supermarket and open the door with her latchkey. He took the key from her, unlocked the door, and carried in the bags.

"Why, Harold," she said, "this is an unexpected pleasure." She had never been sarcastic with him before, and he did not recognize this new note in her voice.

"I'm on the Jagat case," he explained. "Since I was here anyroad, I thought I'd come by and see how you're keeping."

"That's very nice of you, Harold," she said, still in that same mildly amused tone of voice he did not recognize as belonging to his former wife. "Put the bags down in the kitchen, will you. I'll just take off my coat."

The kitchen gave him a shock. He had not been here since the divorce, and scarcely recognized it, with the range cold and dead (reasonably enough, he supposed, since she had just come home from the factory), and a large, new microwave oven taking up a good bit of space. There was a new fridge too, one half of it a freezer. Mavis had always cooked from scratch. He couldn't imagine what she wanted with these new things.

"Funny, you being here," she said, coming back into the kitchen. "The girls wanted to stop at the White Hart for a quick one, but I had a stranger in my cup of tea this afternoon, so I said I'd better come home and see, and here it's only you and not a stranger at all."

"You're looking well, Mavis," he said, for something to say. Her hair, which at the time of the divorce had begun to go gray, was once again the reddish brown of her youth, but it was the hard, monochrome color which comes from a bottle. Her skirt was short, barely touching her knees. Like Beryl she wore high, kick-me-Sadie boots with stiletto heels. Her fat knees bulged over the top like nicely risen popovers. He wished he could keep his mind away from thoughts of food.

Mavis was putting boxes away in the freezer. He said, "I didn't know you'd got a microwave."

"Oh, it's wonderful. You ought to get Beryl one. You just pop a frozen dinner into it, and in a minute you have a hot meal. What about a drink, Harold? You look a bit done in."

"It's been a long day. Ta, yes, I'd love a drink."

She poured them both a gin and lime. The bottle which held the gin was half empty. He wondered if she drank much when she was by herself. "Cheers," he said.

"Cheers."

He felt like a stranger in his own kitchen. At first he had thought it was merely the microwave, but now he realized that the flowers which had bloomed in the window summer and winter had gone. Instead there was a blue plastic vase on the table, holding a blue plastic rose.

"Whatever's happened to all your flowers?" he asked.

"I haven't time to fuss with them now that I'm working."

He could hardly believe it. She'd doted on those flowers, fussed over them as if they had been a pet or a child.

"Do you like it, working?"

"Yes. We have lots of laughs. I wish I'd given it a try years ago. Are you on the case of that actor that got murdered?"

"Jagat. Yes. And I'm not getting anywhere fast. No suspect, no motive anyone can think of. He doesn't seem to have had a single enemy."

"Poor old Harold." She topped up his drink.

Her sympathy stung, but he reminded himself that her judgment had often been remarkably shrewd. Often her common sense had cut through a tangle of useless evidence and shown him the one crucial piece of hidden information. "If we had a motive," he said, "it would be a help. But everyone seems to have liked him. Why would someone kill someone who hasn't an enemy in the world?"

"For the look of things, maybe."

"For what?"

"For the look of things. That's why I would. I can't speak for others."

"I still don't think I follow you, Mavis. What look are you talking about?"

"Being made to look bad, or worse, a fool. Believe me, I know. There was a time I had my kitchen knives good and sharp just in case I ever saw Beryl on a dark night."

She had accepted his request for a divorce so placidly that her sudden vehemence now astonished him. "I didn't know you minded so much," he said. "I'm sorry, Mavis."

"I *didn't* mind. That's what I'm trying to explain to you. I didn't give a damn about you, me, or our marriage. Oh, come on, Harold, don't look so hurt. You didn't either, or you wouldn't have gone off. What had we got left after all those years? We'd nothing to talk about, not even to quarrel, there weren't any kiddies to give us an interest, and you'd be hard put to remember the last time we'd been lovers."

"Missionary position on Saturday night because you could have a lie-in Sunday morning," he said.

Mavis laughed and poured them both another drink. "I realized when I was sharpening my knives that I didn't mind about us at all. What I minded, minded enough to kill, was being made to look ridiculous. I minded those long legs of hers."

"But you didn't kill her. Somebody killed Jagat."

"She was lucky, she was never around at the right time. Of course I've simmered down now, she's quite safe. God gave her her legs and He gave me mine. It's not her fault and it's not mine."

"You're a very smart woman, Mavis."

"I've got smarter. Comes of being alone."

"I still don't think you'd have killed her if you'd come across her on a dark night."

"Don't be too sure of that."

"You think everyone could be a killer, given the right circumstances?"

"Yes, of course. You've only put a thing in the right way. You couldn't have wars else, could you."

"It's a way of looking at it. All right, what combination of circumstances made someone put rat poison in Ally Jagat's gin?"

"How many suspects have you got? Who could actually have got at the gin?"

"Jagat himself, though it's not a nice way to kill yourself, most of the actors, and practically everybody who works at the theater . . . Shrubsole, Barnes . . ."

"Mary Barnes? She might just do it if he'd tracked dirt on her carpet. No, I'm doing Mary an injustice. She's a good soul, even if she is awfully clean."

"The trouble is, all these people more or less alibi each other. Anyone could have poisoned the gin, but there was a lot of coming and going, and someone would most likely have noticed. Verity and her mother carried the table with the drinks on the stage, which means they were the last people near the gin before the curtain went up."

"If you can picture Verity Barnes putting poison in someone's gin you have more imagination than I ever gave you credit for. It's always Mary who has to take the rats out of the traps. Verity can't even stand to look at anything dead. I always said that house so near the tip was a mistake, but there, Mary wanted to be on the High."

"She's got a terrier now. He keeps the rats off, and, she says, she Hoovers him once a day, so he doesn't shed on the furniture.

Mavis laughed loudly at this. "How like Mary. I wouldn't put it past her to Hoover Barnes as well." While they had been talking she had put out glasses and plates. "Some of the girls are coming over after supper to help me watch the telly," she said. "You're welcome to stay, of course."

With an inward shudder at the very idea of "the girls", the inspector said he must be going home. The thought of Constable Gaskell spending another day at the rubbish tip cheered him briefly, but he quickly relapsed into gloom, for he knew, fatally, that after a day on her feet at the hairdresser's where she worked, he would find Beryl all dolled up and ready to dance half the night at the Budgie Cage. And the food the Budgie Cage served didn't bear thinking about. "Oh, I can't get no satisfaction," the Rolling Stones moaned on his car radio. At the moment it struck the inspector as the profoundest philosophy.

CHAPTER V

The memorial service for Algernon was well attended. All the actors were there, of course, as well as the theater staff. Hearing that there were to be refreshments, the Old Age Pensioners had turned out in force, so that the small theater was quickly filled, and a busload of trippers from Scarborough, attracted by newspaper headlines and Tim's appearance on television, was turned away to cool their heels till opening time two and a half hours hence.

"Pity you didn't think to sell tickets," said Gavin Beauclerc to John. "It looks like a smash hit."

"It's disgusting," said John. "I could murder the wretched Selkirk for bringing all that publicity on our heads."

"Dear Ally would have adored it," said Nell Wood, touching a handkerchief to her eyes.

John mounted the stage and looked out over the audience. The townspeople sat modestly in the back rows, most of them dressed in their Sunday churchgoing clothes. The actors, wearing their soberest, were up front, a brighter splash of color. Tim Selkirk wore his usual ruffled shirt, ragged jeans and fringed buckskin jacket. Of course no one wore mourning much nowadays, thought John, except Lady Biggles, who in black tailormades and a Queen Mary toque with a black plume made a striking feature at Rigby funerals. All the same the boy might have made some effort. At the back, standing behind the stalls, he saw Inspector Winterkill, his eyes on the audience rather than on Sir Tancred, who was expressing the deep regret of the board of directors and the management of the theater at the sad death of that talented actor Algernon Jagat. In another moment he would introduce John Silk, saying no doubt, John thought, that he needed no introduction. It occurred to him suddenly that the murderer was very likely in the audience. What did it feel like to attend a memorial service for someone whose gin you had spiked with rat poison? He looked at the rows of faces before him, most of them familiar, yet hardly less revealing than the backs of their heads at which Harold Winterkill was gazing with an air of abstraction. Sir Tancred told his listeners that John Silk needed no introduction, introduced him and turned the stage over to him.

Since at such times the deceased is invariably remembered at his wittiest and kindest, John, paying tribute both to the actor and to his friend, quickly elicited smiles of pleased recollection from those who had known Ally. The townspeople continued to look stern. Rigby still took death seriously, and had a special long face it wore to such occasions. In the wings Baby, Sir Tancred's lurcher, wore exactly the same expression—solemn and sternly disapproving.

"An actor's life is made up of partings and reunions," John said, finishing his brief talk. "When we say goodbye we know that sooner or later there will be another play, another theater somewhere, a film or television serial which will bring us together again. Wherever we are, we shall miss Ally Jagat's voice welcoming us back, we shall miss his inevitable question at such times—'My dear, what is a nice girl like you doing in a place like this?'" The faultless mimicry drew a startled laugh from the actors. For one moment Ally seemed to them not to be lying cold and blue on a mortuary slab, but back in the little Regency theater with them, saying, "It was only a joke, my dears, here I am." Inspector Winterkill saw Mrs. Barnes, who sat at the extreme opposite end of the stalls, go white, and Verity put a comforting arm around her shoulders. He had scarcely known Ally Jagat himself, not being much of a theatergoer, but he and Beryl had watched the Dracula series on the telly, and John Silk's imitation of Jagat's voice had startled him too. Indeed, all the faces he could see looked shocked. The spurts of laughter had come only from the front rows, where the actors sat. But all faces cleared when John Silk wound up his eulogy by saying that thanks to the kindness of Lady Biggle, refreshments would be served in the Green Room for the friends and colleagues of Algernon Jagat. He did not say so out loud, but very much hoped that those who were neither, but had been brought by mere curiosity and sensation seeking, would take the hint and go away.

Lady Biggle, putting a large, black-bordered handkerchief in her bag, looked benignly at the OAPs making for the Green Room before anyone else had the wits to move. "What a very nice talk," she said, shaking John Silk's hand. "Though I must say your imitation of him startled me, it was so very good. It almost seemed for the moment that dear Algernon was back with us. I wish he were. I shall miss him, and he might be able to tell us who his murderer was. It's so very uncomfortable, not knowing."

Others too, John noted, were uncomfortable. Though the Green Room was full with invited and uninvited guests, and everyone, for the sake of politeness, was accepting cups from Mrs. Shrubsole behind the tea urn, or Mrs. Barnes dispensing coffee, no one was touching the food or drink. It was as if they had all suddenly remembered that it was a drink right here, in this very theater, which had killed the person they had gathered to commemorate. John wondered whether he would once again be called upon to take the first mouthful—he was beginning to feel like the foodtasters kings used to keep when they feared being poisoned—when Mr. Oakroyd, accompanied by Ethel and Enid, espied a plate heaped with scones, and without a moment's hesitation, piled high the plates of his two companions and his own, and fell to.

Actors are good at parties. John's team moved among the townspeople and the theater staff, getting everybody talking, leaving behind eddies of subdued laughter and conversation, stirring up the stodgy and bringing out the shy and retiring. Only Tim did not become part of the group, but stood to one side looking lost, the corners of his mouth drooping with self-pity. No one tried to talk to him. Rigby had never approved of him, and undoubtedly his clothes were unsuitable for the occasion, but John noted that his actors too avoided him. He supposed it was simply the social awkwardness of having Tim in the anomalous position of chief mourner—what on earth was one to say to him? Yet he couldn't just be left standing there, something would have to be done. John, feeling tired and sad, wished it weren't up to him to have to do it, but he supposed he owed it to Ally to be civil to the young creature. He began to make his way through the crowd when he realized that he had been forestalled. Verity Barnes had collected a cup of coffee from her mother, and was blushing as she shyly offered it to Tim Selkirk.

John was pleased that she had made the effort to come to the memorial service. He knew that she had been quite ill in reaction to Ally's death—odd, really—had she fancied herself Mina to his Count Dracula?

He watched her offer the cup of coffee and say something: "I'm ever so sorry about your friend," he guessed it would be, his natural gift for mimicry supplying the dialogue he could not hear. Tim thanked her, looking surprised and very grateful that someone had at last taken notice of him. She was a nice girl, Verity, John thought, a "sprigged muslin kind of girl," Ally had called her, and though the Rigby climate rarely allowed anything so light and summery as sprigged muslin, it was easy to see what Ally had meant.

The party was thinning, people stopped to say goodbye, Lady Biggle demanded his attention, Baby, looking soulful, got under people's feet in hopes of leftover scones and cakes, and when John looked over the room again he realized that Verity and Tim had gone. "Together?" he said to Gavin, who had caught his surprised glance.

"Yes. Talk of funeral baked meats."

"Does her mother know? I shouldn't think she'd approve."

"Oh yes. I saw Verity tell her. I dare say she knows Verity will be safe with him."

"All the same . . ."

The telephone rang in his office and he went to answer it. A woman's voice, identifying itself as Constable Stein, asked for Inspector Winterkill. Though he longed to know whether the call had anything to do with Ally, John closed the door on the inspector and returned to the Green Room, where all but the most persistent of the guests were ready to take their leave. John thanked them for coming and saw them to the door, feeling very tired and wishing everyone else would go too. He looked at his watch. A quarter of an hour to opening time. That meant Sir Tancred would be leaving for the White Hart. Lady Biggle, he saw, was being helped into her black coat; even the OAPs, who were making a good job of the last of the cakes, would scarcely outstay the gentry.

The door of his office opened and the inspector came out. "That call was from the medical examiner," he said. "They've finished the P.M."

John, who had only the vaguest idea of what a post-mortem involved, imagined a shelf with neatly ranged jars of formaldehyde, containing bits and pieces of his old friend.

"Did you know he had a bad heart?"

"No. He never mentioned it."

"It was what he died of."

"But everyone said he was poisoned."

"So he was. But it was heart killed him. It's as well, you know. Arsenic takes longer, as a rule, and it's not a pretty way to go. His doctor in London happened to see the story on the telly and rang up the station. Apparently Jagat went to see him not long ago about chest pains. He was told to take things easy and given nitroglycerine pills. It seems there wasn't much else to be done. He might have lived for some years yet, or have gone out in a minute, the doctor said."

" 'For Tim, in case anything should happen to me.' "

"Yes. It was his heart, not some mysterious assassin from his Indian past he was thinking of. Where is the young idiot. I can't wait to see his face when I tell him."

"He's left."

"Pity. I should have liked to be the one to tell him. Bringing the press down on our necks with his lurid fantasies."

"Oh Lord, the press. Some of them are still hopefully hanging about. I rather promised that if they let us have the memorial service without popping flashbulbs in our faces I'd let them know if there was any news. They've kept their side of the bargain. Do you mind if I tell them?"

"No harm in their knowing," said the inspector. It'll all come out at the inquest anyhow. But I would have liked to see young Selkirk's face."

Tim Selkirk, unaccustomed to keeping to the left of the road, was driving fast and badly in a borrowed car, with Verity Barnes by his side. To his surprise she did not seem to be in the least frightened by his terrible driving, but gave every appearance of enjoying the hairbreadth escapes as he nipped around lorries on the wrong side and was loudly cursed by other drivers, confused by his original—or at any rate, American—way of making turns. Her hands covering her eyes, Verity's squeals of terror were those of someone on a roller coaster enjoying her own fear.

"Oh dear," she gasped at one particularly bad corner, "you *are* awful."

"It's not my fault if everybody in England drives on the wrong side of the road."

He did not quite know why he had asked her to dinner. Verity was not the kind of girl he normally noticed, let alone felt any interest in, but when she had approached him with a cup of coffee and her shy condolences, he had felt so out of things, so filled with self-pity at being ignored by everyone, that on an impulse he had said, "Let's get out of this dump. I'll borrow a car and we can drive into Scarborough and have dinner."

She had surprised him by accepting at once. "I'll just tell my mother," she said.

"Call her from Scarborough," he suggested, having a justified suspicion that Mrs. Barnes did not approve of him.

Verity said, "Oh, I could never do that. Don't worry, it'll be all right," and apparently it was, for she had returned to his side almost before he had time to ask Mick (the purveyor of the peyote buttons) whether he could borrow his car.

In a Scarborough pub, Verity, blushing at her own audacity, ordered a sweet sherry—the only drink, aside from christening champagne, she had ever tasted. The Barneses had a small glass of it every Christmas to toast the queen, and though it seemed to her far more daring than driving on the wrong side of the road, she had a sudden wish to seem sophisticated, the way the American girls he knew probably were.

"What did you tell your mother?" Tim asked her after she had taken a small and cautious sip.

"The truth, of course. Well, very nearly the truth. I said some of us were driving into Scarborough to have supper."

"Some of us?"

"Well, you and I are some of us, aren't we?"

They dined at a seaside café on greasy chips and fish encased in a batter so thick it seemed like a battleship afloat on an oil spill. Tim, who had never quite grown accustomed to English food, poked at his plate once or twice and, finding nothing to his purpose, peevishly put it aside. Verity daintily ate every greasy morsel, washing it all down with strong, milky tea.

While Verity ate, Tim talked. The fact that she contributed little to the conversation besides occasional exclamations—"Oh, you are . . ." "Well, I never . . ."—did not trouble Tim, who, having embarked on the enthralling subject of himself was content to shoulder the entire burden of their talk. Verity was not unfamiliar with the world of which he spoke. She had seen American rock festivals and the Chicago student riots on the telly, but she had seen them as remote, as unreal as films and plays. The very unreality of Tim's experience made her unable to recognize much of it as boasting. Nor did she mind that he talked exclusively about himself. It was, even in her limited experience of men, something they usually did.

After dinner they walked through the fun fair and rode the ferris wheel, and when it got dark they climbed the escarpment to the ruins of the castle. They listened to the slap of the water against stone far below them, and looked down at the lights of the town, the garish glow of the amusement arcades, and far out to sea, small as stars, the red and green signals of the fishing boats. The wind was chilly up on the cliff, and Tim, rather reluctantly, put his buckskin coat around Verity's shoulders. They did not talk much, but Tim did not feel uncomfortable. Girls like Verity were mysterious to him, but they presented a mystery he was not interested in probing. He had never learned the polite stages of courtship, the fugitive touch of hands, the first kiss, because the girls he had known had been no more interested in such old-fashioned, unliberated nonsense than he. Most of them had preferred to take charge. If they found him pleasing (as they often did) they would say so, and have him zipped inside their sleeping bags before he had learned more than their first names.

If, on their way down from the castle, he took Verity's hand, it was merely to keep her from stumbling on the steep downgrade. Yet he felt oddly pleased when she did not remove her hand from his once they had reached level ground. He drove home more carefully than he had driven into Scarborough, and delivered Verity at her front door by ten o'clock. He saw a curtain move a discreet inch and knew that Mrs. Barnes had been waiting up for her daughter. "Thanks ever so," said Verity, handing him back his buckskin coat. "It was beautifully warm. I do hope you didn't get cold."

He was cold, and put the jacket on at once. It still held some warmth of Verity's body, and its leather smell mingled with a faint whiff of Yardley's English Lavender.

Mrs. Troutt was still awake when he returned to the room he had shared with Ally. She had in fact stayed up on purpose, wanting to be the first to give him the news that, far from a mysterious assassin stalking Mr. Jagat, he had been killed, as the most humble and pedestrian of us might be, by a weak heart. She had enjoyed having a lodger who was interviewed on the television, but she enjoyed quite as much bringing him back down to the level of ordinary mortals.

It took Tim a long time to get to sleep that night. Though he smoked a joint to make him mellow, and then another, sleep would not come. It was not in his nature to feel remorse, yet what kept him awake was the memory of a night in London, not long before they had come north. Ally had come home that evening, carrying a new bottle of gin and two bottles of wine. He had laughed a good deal, and had tried to get Tim drunk. Tim, who seldom drank more than an occasional glass of beer, preferring his highs from pills and pot, had resisted at first; and Ally, usually the most amiable of companions, had nearly quarrelled with him. "What's the matter," Tim had asked finally. "Are you celebrating something?"

"Oh yes," Ally had said laughing, "I'm celebrating some news I had." They touched glasses. "Cheers," Ally said, not telling him what the news had been. Tim, not all that interested, did not ask. Later they went to eat at the White Elephant, the kind of restaurant Tim's father often went to, but one Ally could ill afford, and later yet Tim was awakened from a drunken sleep to hear Ally sobbing. Tim had had much more wine than he was accustomed to, on top of several martinis. His head hurt and he felt in no mood to listen to Ally's woes. He had pretended sleep, thinking that if Ally was going to become tiresome he might just split. If worst came to worst he could always go back to Daddy, Arabella and Allegra. Then the pretense of sleep became reality, and by the next morning he forgot Ally's tears. Ally was his most charming self, bringing him tea and aspirins in bed, and full of funny hangover stories. Tim had not thought of it from that day to this, but now knew, as surely as if he had sat beside Ally in the doctor's office, that he must have learned the truth that afternoon, must have been told that his heart had betrayed him—not romantically, as it had so often before into the hands of grasping and venal boys, but in its mundane and necessary task of pumping blood and keeping him alive. Ally had wept, that night, knowing that no one else would, certainly not the boy with the fair curls pretending sleep by his side.

"Shit," said Tim, and from the colored assortment of pills in the ashtray he selected two Valiums to alleviate the vague anxiety he did not recognize as the naggings of a bad conscience. "Shit," he said again, but soon the pills did their soothing work. Nothing much mattered after all, Tim thought, and probably the bomb would get them all sooner or later anyway, so why worry? By morning his conscience, never a very active part of his personality, had gone quietly back to sleep, and the only regret he felt was that his time in the light of publicity had been so short. Had he been able to see ahead by just a day or so, to know that his presence in the public glare had scarcely started, he would have been a young man without any regrets whatever.

The inquest brought no new revelations except to those who had missed the news of Ally's heart attack. The medical examiner gave the cause of death as heart failure, and agreed with the coroner's speculation that this might have been brought on by the poison. On the other hand, with a heart in the precarious state of Mr. Jagat's, anything or nothing could have caused the seizure.

"Would the poison have killed him even if his heart had held out," the coroner wanted to know.

The medical examiner said he thought not. "There really wasn't enough to kill a grown, healthy man. He would have been very sick for a few days, but it's unlikely that it would have killed him."

"Have you any idea why the murderer did not use a larger dose?"

"Ignorance, possibly."

"Doesn't it seem more likely that someone ignorant of dosages would have erred on the side of too much rather than too little?"

The medical examiner shrugged and said it was not for him to speculate, simply to give scientific evidence. Mr. Jagat had died of a heart attack. How much, if at all, the poison had played a part in bringing on the attack could not be said.

The heart specialist from London, putting it in more elegant terms, agreed with the medical examiner.

Tim, dressed in his customary ruffled shirt and tight jeans, identified the note, "For Tim, in case anything should happen to me," and the two five-pound notes, answered the coroner's questions of how long had he known the deceased ("seven weeks—indeed"), how they had met ("in a pub, you say?"), and had he known that Mr. Jagat had suffered from a weak heart.

The young medical student, Mrs. Shrubsole and Mrs. Barnes gave their evidence, and Verity, pale but composed, described how they had carried the table with the goblet onto the stage, and how Mr. Jagat had told her to make sure

A Happy English Child

the one with the gin would be closest to his hand. This got a laugh and earned a reprimand from the coroner.

One by one the actors described their positions on the stage; where they had stood and what they had been doing at the moment Mr. Jagat had swallowed his poisoned drink. All the technical stage business was very tedious, and it was close to lunch time; those who were accustomed to being at their favorite pub punctually at opening time were wishing the coroner would get on with it, which he (longing for his pint of Biggles Velvet Stout) did with a brisk verdict of death by heart attack, possibly caused by the administration of arsenic by person or persons unknown.

CHAPTER VI

The fact that Algernon Jagat had died of a heart attack rather than poison took all the fun out of the case as far as the press and the reading public were concerned. There was nothing special in dying of a bad heart; people did so every day. Of course someone had spiked his drink with arsenic, but by the time the evening news came on the television, a popular rock singer had died of an overdose of heroin, a duchess had opened a boutique in Carnaby Street, and a prominent member of the Cabinet had been caught *in flagrante* with a young person of indeterminate gender. Ally's inquest was stale news.

To Rose Church, the reporter from the *Whitby Courant*, this seemed a fearful waste. What on earth was the use of having a perfectly splendid local murder if you couldn't even get a by-line out of it. She went back over her notes to see if any detail of the story might yet be milked for scandal or sensation, and found it almost at once. Daddy—Tim Selkirk's daddy—was Commander Selkirk, extra equerry to the Duke of Edinburgh. Royalty was always front-page stuff, and an extra equerry whose son had been the protégé of a well-known murdered actor—had in other words been living in squalid sin with an aging poofter—and might yet prove to be a suspect, perhaps with luck even the murderer, had to be good for at least one more story.

She telephoned a colleague in London to check out Commander Selkirk's credentials, for she had a shrewd suspicion that Tim Selkirk was not overly given to telling the truth. For once, however, his claim proved to be accurate, and Rose went to her editor with the suggestion that she should follow up the London end of the case. The editor grumpily told her that he hadn't any money to spend on nonsense, and that if she wanted a holiday in London she could bloody well pay for it herself. Rose, not at all surprised, drew a part of her savings out of the post office, put on her sensible tweeds and brogues, and caught an early train south. It was Friday. She would not have to be back at work till Monday morning. By then, who could tell, Rose Church's name might be on the front page of the *Whitby Courant* for all the world—well, for all of Whitby and surroundings—to see.

In London she took a bus to a cheap lodging house in the Caledonian Road, where she had stayed on her only previous visit, and was given a tiny room under the roof. She washed her hands and pulled a comb through her scanty reddish hair. Her face looked spottily at her from the glass. "You'll never be a beauty," she said to it, "but one of these days, Rose Church, you'll be a famous reporter."

Seldom since the days of Horatio Alger has private enterprise and pluck been so promptly rewarded. Rose checked Commander Selkirk's address in the telephone book and set out for Covent Garden. She gazed with lively interest at slim, long-legged girls dressed in the minutest of miniskirts, their eyes painted like those of old time movie vamps, their lips as white as a corpse's. Just such a dazzling creature opened the door at Commander Selkirk's address, asked Rose hospitably to come in, and introduced herself and her equally dazzling female companion. The Commander was not at home just yet, she said, but they were expecting him at any moment.

It was plain to Rose that, though it was by now late afternoon, both girls had only just got out of bed. Their hair hung into their eyes in matted strings, and yesterday's make-up was smeared with sleep. However, they were cheerful and amiable, pressing Rose to have some instant coffee and a cig, and not at all loath to answer her questions. Yes, of course they knew Tim Selkirk, and wasn't it simply awful, his lover being killed like that. Rose asked whether they were Tim's sisters, a question which elicited merry laughter. More like Tim's stepmothers, they said, plainly thinking this a tremendous joke, while it slowly dawned on Rose that Allegra and Arabella must be Commander Selkirk's mistresses. "Oh, thank you, God," she thought, seeing a front-page story take shape, while Allegra and Arabella prattled happily away about everything and nothing: clothes, boys, films, their jobs —modelling, they said. Knowing that for girls like themselves there can be no such thing as bad publicity, they showed her pictures of themselves, as unembarassed as if they had been of a naked baby on a bear skin. Rose, blushing but game, said, "I thought you meant fashion modelling." They assured her that fashion was of all things what they wanted to do, unless they got fearfully lucky and landed on the telly or in the films. Well, yes, they had done films, but there again, clothes hardly came into it.

"Did Tim model too?" Rose asked, shocked.

"Oh yes, he had a lovely bod," they told her, and brought out photographs to prove it.

Rose, who had found it embarassing enough to look at the snaps of the girls in their natural state, shut her eyes, but kept her composure sufficiently to ask whether she might have some of the pictures.

"Are you gone on Tim, then?" they asked sympathetically. "We were too, at first, he does look so smashing, but he's a bit dim, don't you think?"

Rose said she hardly knew him. "It wouldn't do me any good if I were gone on him, would it," she said.

"Oh, I don't know," said Arabella (or Allegra). "Tim's not a bit particular." Hearing herself, she put a hand over her mouth and said, "Oh dear, I am sorry, Rosie. I didn't mean it the way it sounded. I only meant that Tim doesn't really mind whether you're a boy or a bird."

Rose digested this information in silence. Arabella and Allegra, who looked as slender as if they lived on nothing but honeydew, suddenly decided that they were starving. Without bothering to comb their hair, or wash their smeary, enchanting faces, they went out and returned in a very short time with newspapers filled with greasy fish and chips, which they washed down with the Commander's Château Latour. The Commander, who arrived as they were halfway through their meal, said mildly, "Darlings, wouldn't the plonk have done as well," greeted Rose very pleasantly, excused himself while he changed out of his uniform into jeans and an embroidered shirt, and settled down on the floor to roll joints for all of them. Rose, who had been very strictly brought up, was not used to wine and had drunk only a few sips. Even so, her head felt strangely light, and wishing to keep her brain clear, she refused the joint offered her.

"Did you know Algernon Jagat?" she asked the Commander.

"Not personally. Why, do you think I killed him?"

"No, of course not," said Rose, to whom the thought had in fact occurred that a father might wish to rescue his son from a life of perversion by any means including murder. But that, of course, had been before she had set eyes on Commander Selkirk, Allegra and Arabella.

"Didn't you mind him living with Mr. Jagat?" Rose asked.

"No, why should I?"

"Well, he is your son."

"Yes, technically I suppose that's so. But I hardly knew him. He turned up here one day, having quarrelled with his mother—my former wife. I hadn't seen him since he was quite small, but I found him rather agreeable."

"Do you think *he* could have killed Mr. Jagat?"

Commander Selkirk thought this over with his usual detachment. "I suppose he might have. But what would have been the point? If he'd grown tired of Jagat he could have simply left him. He knew he could always come back here."

Arabella, whose long, graceful legs were disposed across the Commander's lap, said, "I don't think he could have killed him, you know. Not Tim. Not like that. Tim might kill someone accidentally, give them too many pills, or mix them the wrong way. But anything that needed planning and timing, no, I really don't think so. Tim was a duck, but let's face it, he wasn't very organized."

"True," Commander Selkirk agreed. "On life's chandelier, Tim is not the brightest bulb."

Arabella began to laugh at this. The Commander tickled the soles of her bare and rather dirty feet. A dreary late afternoon pressed against the windows. Allegra drew the curtains and turned on a dim red light. Music pulsed much too loudly from an elaborate stereo set. A joss stick spread sweet but not unpleasant incense clouds through the room. Rose accepted a glass of the plonk Allegra had fetched from the kitchen, and later tried a puff from the joint made with Commander Selkirk's best Acapulco Gold. Later some people came, several young men and women who sat or lay about on the floor. Someone brought Chinese food and wine, someone else offered a bag of cocaine. Rose, feeling mellow, somehow protected by the noisy music, the strange dim light, and the fact that she didn't know any of these people, puffed a little more of the Commander's joint, and accepted another glass of wine. The evening grew more and more dreamlike. One of the young men asked her to dance, and later she found herself on the bed with him without quite knowing how she had got there. She woke in the small hours of the morning, finding that she was sharing the bed not only with her original young man, but with Commander Selkirk and Arabella, none of whom had any clothes on. Nor, for that matter, had she. Her head ached abominably, her stomach churned. Crawling on the floor, trying to find her clothes, sent rockets of pain through her sinuses. She found a bathroom where she was sick, dressed with shaking hands, brushed her teeth with someone else's toothbrush, and cautiously made her way past the entwined sleepers and out the door. The fresh air made her feel better. A taxi took her at tremendous expense to her rooming house, where she fell at once asleep. By morning—such was her sturdy Yorkshire constitution—she felt much better, and a nice hot breakfast of bacon, eggs, boiled tomato and cast-iron tea restored her entirely to her normal self. She had a strong suspicion that in the course of last night she had lost her virginity, and wondered how and to whom. Though she no longer accepted the rigid teachings of her parents' religion, she thought it might be a good idea to go to church. There was one in the little park by the Crescent, the landlady said. A bit low, but very nice.

Rose thought low would suit her penitential morning-after mood. But as she opened her purse to take out her gloves, her fingers encountered the photos so kindly given her by last night's hostesses. In a moment she forgot all about church, and remembered only that, if she had lost her virginity, she had gained a tremendous, a truly mind-boggling story. Oh my hat, yes! *"Father of Murder Suspect in Covent Garden Love Nest.* Commander Niall Selkirk, extra equerry to the Duke of Edinburgh, father of Tim Selkirk, intimate companion of the late Algernon Jagat, whose unsolved murder . . ." Oh my hat yes, never mind church, sorry God, and thank you a million times, Arabella and Allegra, thank you all so very, very much.

CHAPTER VII

John Silk stared disgustedly at the papers displayed at a Scarborough newsstand. In headlines so large as to be nearly unreadable, *SLY* announced the first instalment of Commander Selkirk's memoires of life at Buckingham Palace, while *PRY*, its rival to the death, promised its readers yet more photographs of Arabella and Allegra in the altogether.

From the day Rose Church had sold her story (with illustrations) to *PRY*, until now, three weeks later, a breathless public had been able to follow the adventures of Commander Selkirk, Arabella, Allegra, Tim, and the assorted free spirits who visited them in their "pad." Commander Selkirk's living arrangements were spread over every available front page, there were special pull-out sections dealing with drugs, nudity and general depravity in royal circles, though as the Commander said to one of the many interviewers and photographers who besieged the door of the Covent Garden flat, no one could call dear Allegra and Arabella royal circles.

The two girls were delirious with joy. Their pictures were moved from the centerfolds of various sleaze magazines to the covers of high-fashion journals. There was talk of film contracts and television shows. Commander Selkirk had been frostily requested to turn in his resignation and Buckingham Palace parking sticker, which he did without regret, seeing that he had already signed a book contract with serialization rights in *SLY* and such subsidiary and overseas rights as would keep him in Acapulco Gold and Château Latour for many years to come.

The fact that a man had been brutally murdered, and that the murderer was still at liberty, had been quite forgotten.

Inspector Winterkill, who happened to be passing, stopped, shook his head over the headlines on display, and said, "It's just opening time. Come and have a drink."

"I don't think I'd better," said John. "I'm in a vile mood."

The inspector looked once more at the headlines and said, "I expect they'll get tired of it after a bit."

"You have an optimistic disposition."

"No one who's been on the force as long as I have has an optimistic disposition. People do get tired of things. These days, what with the papers and the telly and everybody hashing over the same thing, they get tired of it faster than ever. Even the second coming wouldn't be a nine days' wonder these days."

"Everyone got tired of Ally's murder awfully fast, that I grant you," John agreed.

"Is that what's got you into such a vile mood?"

"Why not? Without this stupid Selkirk business we might have kept the murder of a well-known actor in the public eye a little longer. It doesn't seem fair that Ally should be forgotten because some silly girls take their clothes off for photographers, as if that were news."

"We haven't forgotten, Silk," said the inspector, not speaking very truthfully, for while Algernon Jagat's name was still on the books as an unsolved murder, the police, being busy with many other things, had let it slip to the back of the drawer.

They found an agreeable-looking pub which was not too full of trippers. The inspector went to the bar for drinks and returned with a pint of ale for himself, a small dry sherry for John, and a bag of crisps which John, with a shudder he hoped was merely inward, refused.

"It's better for us really when the public attention's no longer on a case," said the inspector after a deep drink of his ale. "That's when people start getting careless and make mistakes."

"It looks like the carelessness of the murderer is about all we can bank on."

"At the moment. It's odd, not having any suspects at all, but there it is. Young Selkirk's the likeliest, from our point of view, though really only because lads like him so often do turn nasty. But he has no motive, at least not one we know about, and though he may have had the opportunity, he was, according to everyone who saw him, in no shape to take advantage of it. Could he have faked being sick?"

"He's not much of an actor. And according to the ambulance people, who ought to know, he was, as they put it, very definitely wrecked."

The inspector laughed. "Yes. They have plenty of experience these days, with all those rock concerts. Who else? The fair Shrubsole?"

"Few things would please me more. But what motive could she possibly have had?"

"Pure venom. She can't abide wogs and poofters, and poor Jagat was both."

John hated to see his friend relegated to the army of "poor so and so," but supposed it was part of the indignity of being dead. "If you can build a case on that," he said, "I shall be most grateful. Death or prison are about the only chances that will ever rid me of Mrs. Shrubsole."

"None of the actors had a motive. What about the staff?"

"The Barneses? The little chap couldn't hurt a fly. And can you picture Verity poisoning someone? Besides, the same thing holds true of them as it does of the others. No motive."

"You didn't mention Mrs. Barnes."

John hesitated. Then he said, "I don't for a moment think she did it. The same holds true of her as of everyone else we have discussed. She had the opportunity—indeed, she was last on the stage with the drinks—but again she hadn't a serious motive."

The inspector picked up his empty glass. John, who had barely sipped his sherry, took the hint, said "My turn," and went to the bar.

"When you say no serious motive," said the inspector when John returned, "what un-serious motive did you have in mind?"

"Well, I was thinking of Verity. She had a bit of a thing about Ally. Quite harmless, of course, but she'd seen his Dracula, and like many another pure English maiden she was carried away by those sensuous fangs."

The inspector laughed. "Beryl, my wife, was just the same. She wouldn't even answer the telephone while it was on. And if you knew Beryl you'd know what that means. If there's anything to those theories of acquired characteristics, the next generation ought to be born with a telephone permanently wedged between the left collarbone and ear."

"I shouldn't be surprised. The thing is, you know, I can picture Mrs. Barnes committing a murder. I'm speaking from a theater point of view, of course. No one would cast Verity as a poisoner unless it was to mislead the audience to the end, but you could cast her mother. I think if she had a strong motive—Verity's virtue being one—she would be capable of murder."

The inspector emptied the last of the crisps from the packet into his mouth. "Tracking dirt on the carpet," he said indistinctly.

"Sorry?"

He swallowed and, his speech now unimpeded, said again, "Tracking dirt on the carpet. It's something Mavis—my ex-wife—said when we talked about the case. Mavis thinks anyone can be made to commit murder, given the right circumstances. You couldn't have wars else, according to her. And she said if you tracked dirt on Mary Barnes's carpet, metaphorically speaking, that might make her capable of murder. It wasn't meant seriously, of course."

"Of course."

"Besides, Mary wouldn't worry about Jagat. Her having been a landlady, she'd know about his sort, so she wouldn't give it a thought, if you see what I mean."

"Yes, of course. I didn't know Mrs. Barnes had ever been a landlady."

"Kept a bed-and-breakfast in Brighton after the war. They didn't come back to Rigby until after Verity was born."

"There goes another suspect. Tell me, what do you look for, now, three, four weeks after the murder. Whatever clues there may have been surely have been tidied away by now."

The inspector sighed, his face glum. There were precious few clues, tidied or not. The gin bottle had never been found. County Forensic had gone through every bit of rubbish from the theater thought capable of having held the poison, and, with even less enthusiasm, had fingerprinted a large sack full of poison-pen letters cut from the Sunday papers and glued on cheap stationery. The prints were sticky and beautifully clear, and almost all of them belonged to small children. The few which were those of grown-ups were not on record, and doubtlessly were the property of blameless and long-suffering parents helping their bored offspring to pass a long rainy Sunday afternoon.

"Well, clues, you know . . ." said the inspector, dismissing them. "What you look for now is changes in behavior, a break in the pattern. After a time the guilty party starts to feel safe and relax. Thieves begin to throw their money about, murderers suddenly find a will no one had known existed, leaving all the boodle to them."

"Ally didn't have much to leave."

"No, apparently not. I only gave it as an example. You look for oddities, things that don't fit. Is anyone acting differently from the way they acted before? Well, I have to be going. I promised Beryl to take her to see *The Graduate*, and she'll have my head on a plate if I'm late."

The inspector left. John remained seated alone at the table, considering the members of his theater company. Was anyone behaving oddly? Not really. All the actors except Bertie, from whom it could not be expected, had rallied to put aside personal jealousies and ambitions and close the gap Ally's death had left. The theater had never done so well—it sold out every night—though that was due, John knew, not to a thirst for art, but to morbid curiosity and the fond hope that the murderer might strike again.

Nell Wood had taken over the part of Lady Bracknell, and was doing unexpectedly well by it. Ally had been one of her dearest and oldest friends, but despite the great distress his murder had caused her, she had not relapsed into drink. John was grateful for her sobriety, and hoped she would get over a streak of bad luck which had been dogging her over these last weeks. He had seen this before in people who had given up drink; for a time they became extraordinarily accident-prone. While they were still on the sauce, walking, as the French so felicitously put it, on round feet, they might topple like a baby, or bump into things, but they could pick themselves up as if nothing had happened. He'd seen Nell, so drunk she could barely stand, weave her way across Trafalgar Square in patterns that were as erratic as they were successful. Yet now, when she was being so sober and good, she was as bruised and banged about as an unsuccessful boxer.

On the morning of Ally's funeral she had tripped on a loose bit of drugget and fallen down a flight of stairs in her lodgings. During the performance of *An Inspector Calls* the heel had come off one of her shoes and she had sprained her ankle so badly she had to act with a cane for a week. Finally the leg of a chair had broken as she had plopped herself into it in the role of Lady Bracknell. Barnes had been extremely annoyed about that. The chair with the wobbly leg had been put aside by him personally, to be mended; it wasn't his fault, he said, if some damned fool of an American had put it back on the stage. For such a mousy little man he had become quite voluble, for the damned fool was Tim Selkirk, who had been helping Verity set the stage, and Barnes had no liking for that young man.

Tim Selkirk?

Was it out of character for him to have stayed on in Rigby after the inquest? And if so, was it a sign of guilt or innocence? Would a guilty person have breathed a sigh of relief on hearing the words, "Person or persons unknown," and have hurried back to London to lose himself among the crowds of a large city? Or was he brazening it out in Rigby, hoping the police would take it as a sign of a tranquil conscience?

Did his having been Ally's lover constitute a motive for murder? John thought not. He had not seen enough of the two of them together to judge how happy or quarrelsome a menage it had been, but he found it difficult to take it seriously enough to envisage a crime of passion.

Tim had an alibi, for what it was worth, and no known motive. Was he a person even capable of committing murder? John doubted it but could not be sure. He simply did not understand people of Tim Selkirk's sort. They came his way frequently, because they tended to drift toward the theater—or, more often, films and television—but their general vagueness and want of direction were so puzzling to John that they precluded his understanding anything about them at all. It wasn't a question of the generation gap one read so much about in the papers these days. John had no problem understanding young people like Nigel and Gavin, who were really no different from what he had been at their age: ambitious, hard-working, knowing exactly who and what they wanted to be. Tim Selkirk, Mick, and some of the others dabbled at this or that, drifting through each day, thinking vaguely, if they thought at all, that they might awaken one fine morning to discover that overnight they had been transformed into Mick Jagger. And while John deplored Mick Jagger both for the unattractiveness of his face and the truly dreadful noise his band made, he suspected that Mr. Jagger had worked very hard for his success, something that neither Tim nor any of his friends seemed inclined to do.

He found it difficult to imagine anyone so dim and undefined as Tim planning and committing a murder. Most likely he was just staying on because his friend Mick always knew where to get drugs, and he thought Verity a pretty girl.

Verity Barnes had been ill for days after Ally's death, but there was nothing out of the ordinary about that. She'd had a schoolgirl crush on Ally, and being present at the sudden death of someone she adored would account for it easily. Was the friendship with Tim Selkirk an odd thing for her? They seemed to be spending a great deal of time together since they had gone to dinner after the memorial service for Ally. At that time Verity had probably thought of Tim as lonely and mournful, and having been Ally's boy, no danger to her virginity. Out of a natural generosity of heart she had offered him her company. But Rose Murphy's revelations of the goings-on *chez* Commander Selkirk, not to mention the magazines and porn films, suggested a world Verity Barnes could hardly consider acceptable. Yet she had not broken with Tim. There was something of a mystery there, but the mystery might well consist simply of the fact that Tim Selkirk had fair curls and a pretty face.

Far odder, surely, was the fact that Mrs. Barnes had taken no serious steps to put an end to their friendship. True, when the stories about Tim, Allegra and Arabella had first spilled from *SLY* and *PRY* into the daily papers, Mrs. Barnes and Verity had had a quarrel about Tim. This had happened at the theater, in the prop room, and though the door had been closed, voices were raised, and a good deal of the quarrel was overheard by some of the actors.

"I know it's not polite to eavesdrop," Nell Wood said, telling John about it later. "But a disagreement between Verity and her mother is so astonishing, I'm afraid we all cast good manners to the winds and listened for all we were worth."

John, who felt strongly that it was not polite to listen to gossip, found himself quite unable to resist the baser part of his nature. "What exactly happened?" he asked.

"I didn't hear the beginning," said Nell. "I expect la Barnes read about dear Tim's doings in London and told Verity not to see him again. And Verity, most surprisingly, refused. First love, I expect. Surely no other emotion could be powerful enough to make Verity stand up to her mother."

"What did Mrs. Barnes say to that?"

"Oh, the sort of things mothers do say at such times. 'You'll do as I tell you, miss, or your dad'll take the strap to you . . .'"

"That I cannot believe."

"Well, I'm giving you the spirit of the thing, not the exact words. Voices had got fairly high by then, so this bit is verbatim: Verity said, 'You know why I'm going to keep on seeing Tim, and you know why you can't stop me.'"

"I can't believe it. Verity!"

"Neither could we. But what was even more incredible, Johnny, was that Mrs. B. caved in. Oh, she mumbled something about a serpent's tooth and sniffed a bit, but that was the end of the quarrel. She simply gave up. Isn't it odd?"

It was odd, very odd, truly out of the pattern, the one break in behavior of which the inspector had spoken. A young, strictly brought up girl like Verity might be secretly intrigued by the revelations of Tim's past, she might even think them romantic, but Mrs. Barnes, a strict chapel-goer, possessed of the worldly wisdom of a former landlady, would have no romantic notions about the likes of Tim Selkirk. Yet she had "caved in" and her only and much loved daughter continued to go about with a very unsavory young man.

Why? It hardly proved that she had murdered Ally, but it did allow for a certain amount of speculation.

Out of all the people he and Inspector Winterkill had

talked about, she was the only one he could picture committing a murder. Moreover he could without difficulty picture her committing that kind of murder. "Tracking dirt on the carpet," Mavis Winterkill had said. Yes, he could see Mrs. Barnes killing for respectability's sake. A woman who would buy a house adjoining a rubbish tip for the sake of a High Street address might remove someone who threatened her family's good name, as casually as she killed the rats that infested her cellar, and kill him with the same poison.

The pub had filled up while John had been sitting, thinking things over, and he suddenly caught the reproachful eye of the barmaid on his scarcely touched sherry. He was taking up a seat and not drinking. Guiltily he bought a large Scotch to make up for his dereliction, and sipped it absently while he returned to thoughts of Mrs. Barnes.

Two problems made nonsense of his suspicions. First of all, the Barnes family was almost ostentatiously respectable; sober chapel people, downright boring with their lack of even the least touch of scandal. And had there been such a thing, and had Ally known of it (most unlikely since, as far as John knew, he had never set eyes on the Barneses until he had come to Rigby), Ally would have been the very last person in the world to make use of such information, to—the very thought was ludicrous—blackmail someone.

Yet Mrs. Barnes had lodged herself in his mind and would not let go. He lay awake hours that night, turning possibilities over in his mind, scarcely noticed that he had eaten all three pieces of his Melba toast for breakfast, and that the *Rigby Sentinel*, never the most enthralling of journals, had been read from cover to cover without a single story having stuck in his mind.

Brighton. The Barneses had kept a bed-and-breakfast hotel in Brighton. Had something happened there that they wanted to keep secret? Was that why they had sold up and returned to Rigby, to work for someone else at menial jobs when they had owned their own business? Had Ally ever been to Brighton? John could not recall him mentioning it, but surely he might have. Everyone had been to Brighton at some time or another.

He wondered what their bed-and-breakfast place had been called. That at least would be simple enough to learn. Finding Barnes alone, engaged on a piece of carpentry, John stopped to ask his advice. He had to go to Brighton to have a look at an actor who might do to replace Ally Jagat. He understood that Barnes knew Brighton. Could he recommend a place to stay?

Barnes put down his tools and considered. The time of year was the trouble, he said. In August Brighton would be full to the last cubbyhole and bathtub. He and Mrs. Barnes had once owned a bed-and-breakfast place there, that was how he knew. The Hotel Wellington, it was called. He might try there, though it had always been full in the summer in the days he and Mrs. Barnes had run it. There was a place next door that was more likely to be able to accommodate him. The trouble was he couldn't put his tongue to the name at the moment. Something to do with the Himalayas—there'd been a film about it. It would come back to him if he didn't worry at it.

John suggested that a pint at the Theater Pub might help. Barnes looked around cautiously to make sure that neither his wife nor Lola Shrubsole were on the premises, and said he didn't mind if he did. Over his beer he talked happily about his days in Brighton, and the problems of running a bed-and-breakfast hotel, but it was all small domestic detail, the clogged drains and sticking drawers stuff of daily boarding-house life. But at least the pint lubricated his memory. He now recalled what the bed-and-breakfast place next door was called: the Shangri La.

CHAPTER VIII

"Listen, it's a moor hen."

"What is?"

"Listen. You can hear it plain as plain. 'Get back, get back.'"

"Get back where?"

Verity began to laugh. "Silly. That's what a moor hen call sounds like. As if it were saying 'Get back, get back.'"

Tim listened. Presently the moor hen repeated her call. "That's amazing," said Tim. "Really amazing."

Verity was busy gathering bilberries into her handkerchief. Tim looked at the horizon and the distant sea. The dales fell away from him like giant dunes, golden and purple with heather, their slopes marked out with endless stone walls that caused a fugitive wonder in the mind at the patience that had labored to build them.

Here and there, in the folds of the dales, beekeepers stood guarding the hives they had brought to the moor to gather, Verity had told him, the bitter heather honey much prized by the local inhabitants. It seemed to Tim an odd thing to bring bees out here, like taking a dog for a walk. "Don't they ever get lost?" he asked her.

"No, never. Isn't it lovely today?" Verity settled down beside him. "Have some berries." They had stained her handkerchief.

"You should have used a tissue," Tim said, taking a berry. "Say, these are good. What are they?"

"Bilberries. Don't you have them in America?"

"I don't know. I don't think so."

Verity took a berry and put it daintily in her mouth. Then

she leaned back against the sun-warmed wall of a wooden shed. This shed, built originally in World War II to shelter aircraft spotters from the cutting winds sweeping over the dales, now served as a shelter only for lovers. Rigby, well aware of the use it was put to, had periodically debated pulling it down, but its demolition would have cost too much, and Rigby, weighing the expense against the sin, decided each time to leave well enough alone.

Tim finished the last of the berries and settled himself beside Verity, sliding an arm beneath her head. She turned to him at once, both eager and shy, and they began to kiss.

People who had wondered why Tim had stayed on in Rigby tended to discount Verity as a reason. She was pretty, of course, and very sweet, but she was surely not Tim's type, and there was no denying that her conversation was decidedly dim.

Yet Verity was indeed the reason Tim had stayed on in Rigby. The fact that Inspector Winterkill had said, "You won't go anywhere without letting us know, will you," had long since slipped his mind. He had, quite simply, fallen in love for the first time in his life. Probably his feelings could more accurately be described as infatuation, but they were all the more intense for that.

It was not in Tim to be analytical about his feelings, or indeed anyone else's. When Verity had brought him a cup of coffee after Ally's memorial service, she had touched him at a rare moment of loneliness and introspection. When she had agreed to come out to dinner with him he had been flattered. Here at last was someone who took him at his own valuation. John Silk and the members of his acting company were always perfectly polite, but he sensed obscurely that for them he did not really exist, carried no weight. Verity not only took him seriously, she admired him and was even a little afraid of him.

Her kisses were as ardent as they were inexperienced. She smelled of lavender, shampoo, and very slightly of sweat.

Tim was not put off by this. The women students at Berkeley, who refused on feminist principle to shave their armpits or use deodorants, had smelled much worse.

His own kisses, as eager as hers, and far more experienced, were by now meant to be a diversionary tactic. But, as always before, just as his hands were about to have their way, Verity, breathing as if she had just finished a race, pulled away and said no.

Tim had no experience of girls like Verity, and therefore none either of the graduated steps of seduction. The girls at Berkeley had been only too ready to push him down and climb on top. Until Verity he had never experienced the intense pleasure and agony of extended foreplay with no resolution.

"Oh, Verity," he groaned, "it's killing me. Please, please let me."

But Verity was not to be talked into anything. Her virginity was a tangible asset to her, like the money in her post-office savings book. Both would some day be surrendered to the fortunate man who took Verity to the altar. She might be dim, but she was no fool, and no matter how fast Tim's hands made her heart beat, she knew he was not that man.

"Are you afraid of me, Verity? Because of all those stories in the paper? I wouldn't hurt you, I promise."

She shook her head. "Of course not, silly."

She had accepted the revelations about him in the placid manner of those who did not read newspapers for news but for "human interest," and take scandal and suffering in high places as their due. She did not grudge the rich and famous their success, money, limousines, palaces, meals in expensive restaurants, but in return for these perks she expected to read about their drunkenness, drug addiction, sexual irregularity and profligacy, despair and suicide.

It was not that she was unkind or callow, but that the glamorous creatures who drunkenly wrecked their cars or took too many pills were like the people who appeared in two dimensions, in black and white on her family's television screen. That Tim had lived in that world impressed and excited her, but the Tim who had disported himself with Allegra and Arabella was no more real to her than the black and white photographs or the shadowy actors on a screen.

Tim had attempted to explain to her the theories of Professor Norman O. Brown, theories which in Tim's version of them became the simple sexual ethic of "whatever floats your boat, baby." Verity was not impressed. Her mother had taught her that all through history men have invented similar theories, all of which, however high-sounding they might be, had the simple and single-minded aim of getting inside a girl's knickers. She wasn't having any of it.

Tim held her tightly and groaned. The customary masculine ploys—"If you loved me you wouldn't reject me, you've got me into this condition, it's up to you to do something about it . . ."—did not come readily to his tongue, for he had never had occasion to rehearse them. All he could do was to threaten to go back to London, a city full of girls like Arabella and Allegra, who did not know the word no. Verity sighed, but accepted his threat with her usual good sense, agreeing sadly that it might be best for both of them.

"I can get to third base," Tim said to John, "but I don't get to score."

To John's dismay the boy had lately taken to visiting him, and frequently bored him with his callow and valueless opinions. Of late his struggle with Verity's virtue had been the main topic of conversation. John felt this to be both tasteless and embarrassing, but Tim, not sensitive to finer shades, talked past John's silences and fastidious expression.

"I have never been able to feel passionate about cricket," John said now, "and I must confess that baseball is *terra incognita* to me, but I think I get your drift."

Tim looked at him with his attractive smile. "Wow! You

talk just like a professor I had at Berkeley. I couldn't understand half of what he said."

John wondered whether Tim was capable of mockery, but no: His smile was wholly one of admiration. On occasions such as these John found himself briefly, very briefly, liking the boy.

"Why not leave the girl alone," he said. "I gather from the papers that virgins are about to be an endangered species. It will be interesting to have one at Rigby Rep."

"You don't know how I feel, John," Tim groaned. "It's awful. I guess I could hit her over the head and get her that way, but that's not what I want. I want her to feel about me the way I feel about her."

"That's nice of you," John said drily, but Tim was content to take his words at face value.

"Could I ask you something, John? Something kind of private?"

"You may ask. I may not answer."

"When you were young, were all the chicks virgins?"

Thanks to many years in the theater, John was able to keep a straight face. "If they were not, they pretended to be. But I rather think a good many of them were."

"How'd you talk them out of it?"

"Oh, we were romantic in those days." Though he was only fifty-one, talking to Tim always made John feel as old as Anchises. "We quoted poetry. 'Had we but world enough and time, this coyness, lady, were no crime.' That one always worked very well, as I remember."

Tim looked up, startled. His English professor at Berkeley, driven by the manic optimism which causes people to become teachers in the first place, had, back in Tim's student days, attempted to insert a modicum of poetry into minds which, if they contained anything at all, were cluttered with rock lyrics, revolutionary slogans, and exhortations to expand their perceptions in words of no more than one syllable. Tune in, turn on, drop out.

Yet poetry is insidious and will tunnel its way into minds not disposed to receive it. During pot-smoking sessions one or the other line from some masterpiece of English verse would suddenly surface in Tim's stoned mind. "I grow old . . . I grow old . . . I shall wear the bottoms of my trousers rolled," would take on the magic property of an incantation, while "deserts of vast eternity" had caused him to shiver with superstitious awe and exclaim "Like wow!" in youthful admiration.

With the excellent memory which is one of the benefits of the uncluttered mind, Tim found himself recalling a good part of the Marvell poem. "Like, I know that one," he said to John. "We had this old crock of a professor who was always making us read stuff like that. Wasn't there a line about 'worms shall try that long preserved virginity'? Maybe I should try that on Verity."

"Yes," said John. "It goes on:

> And your quaint honour turn to dust
> And into ashes all my lust.
> The grave's a fine and private place,
> But none, I think, do there embrace."

"Wow," said Tim, thinking it over. "When a friend of mine got married, they read Kahlil Gibran, but this is even better. The only thing is, Verity'd never believe it. I mean, like, world enough and time's the one thing I got lots and lots of."

CHAPTER IX

Every room in Brighton was filled with tourists. The bed-and-breakfast hotels along the pleasant street where the Wellington was located, all flourished NO VACANCY signs above their bright window boxes—all, that is, but one: the Shangri La. John realized at once why Barnes had been so confident of his finding a room there. The Shangri La was a bed-and-breakfast hotel of last resort. In his younger acting days, touring the provinces, John had stayed in hundreds of them, and knew without so much as peeking into a window exactly what he would find. From the dusty plastic flowers in the window boxes, and the straggling weeds in the garden, he knew all he wanted to know about the landlady though, until he rang the bell, he could not be sure whether she would be the run-down, cosy kind, her ample form imperfectly contained in a flowered overall, or the stringy sort with over-permed, dyed hair in rollers. He knew the stairs would be steep and narrow, and that on the low landing there would be a sign saying: MIND YOUR HEAD!!! The bedroom would be small, filled with wobbly furniture, while a fixed basin would leak with the steady "drip drip" of the Chinese water torture into a tin pail. The "conveniences" would consist of a tub with most of its enamel scrubbed off, and a loo that was not scrubbed often enough. That was the "bed" part. He did not feel strong enough as yet to contemplate the "breakfast."

The landlady, Mrs. Drabble, was the scrawny sort, with curlers in her hair and a cigarette stuck in the corner of her mouth. Yes indeed she had a room, she said, and with a defiant look at the neighboring houses with their freshly painted shutters, sparkling windows, burgeoning flower boxes and ubiquitous NO VACANCY signs, she took down her own ROOMS TO LET, turned it to the pristine side which proclaimed NO VACANCIES and hung it back on its nail. John followed her inside, up the steep and narrow stair, minded his head, was coyly shown the little landing which contained the bathroom and the lav, and entered a room which so exactly matched his expectations of it that he almost laughed out loud.

"This will do me very well, Mrs. Drabble," he said. "Would you like me to pay for it now?"

Though her eyes lit up at the mention of money, she told him there was no hurry. He followed her downstairs to sign the book.

"There now," she said, reading over his shoulder, "if it isn't a small world. Rigby, Yorks. Believe it or not, I've got a friend there. Mary Barnes her name is. She used to own the Wellington next door."

"It's a small world indeed," John agreed. "Mrs. Barnes works for me now, or rather, I should say, for the Rigby Repertory Company."

"Would you be a theatrical, then? I've had them staying here many a time."

Not during their more prosperous years, thought John, explaining who he was.

"You had a murder there," Mrs. Drabble suddenly remembered. "It's just come back to me. An actor, right on the stage." Her pleasure at having someone in her house connected with a recent murder was indecent to see. Much as he would have liked to talk with her about Mary Barnes's years in Brighton, John felt too nauseated to stay in the same room with her. Though it was raining lightly, he said he thought he would go for a walk.

The little antique shops in the Lanes soothed him, though everything was priced for the American tourist trade, and the exquisite Georgian desk, which would have fitted so beautifully into his hexagonal sitting room in Rigby, displayed a price tag that removed it from any realistic consideration. The Beatles informed him from a radio in an open window that they had no money either, but they seemed quite cheerful about it since, they pointed out to him, money could not buy you love. Reflecting that it could buy Georgian desks, John removed himself from temptation and walked along the Front, where he observed damp, sandy children being cross, while their equally damp and sandy mothers displayed the determined good cheer that is bred into the inhabitants of a country where the summers are usually both cold and wet. "We've paid all this money," they seemed to be saying, "and we are going to enjoy ourselves, by God."

If John had hoped to have a talk with his landlady this very evening, he was to be disappointed. Mrs. Drabble, her husband and a neighboring couple sat bathed in the bluish light of the television set. "You're very welcome to join us in the lounge, Mr. Silk," Mrs. Drabble said, not turning her eyes from the screen, and John, seeing that he would not win her attention again that night, thanked her and went to his room.

The next morning was better. Breakfast was very much as he had expected, served in a steamy cellar room on tables covered with American oilcloth. Drabble was at the stove in the adjoining kitchen, frying bacon, but Mrs. Drabble was serving breakfast and chatting cordially with her guests, all of them Americans, as John could tell from the volumes of *Europe on $10.00 a Day* by their plates. He was offered a choice of sausage and tomato or eggs and bacon, asked for tea and toast and got exactly what he expected; four half slices of damp leather cooling in a metal rack, melting pats of New Zealand butter wrapped in foil, and a glass bowl of marmalade which contained not even the vestige of an orange peel. The tea was so black that the Americans, who had foolishly asked for coffee, looked at it in wonder, plainly wishing their coffee had achieved an equally dusky shade.

They went off, clutching their *$10.00 a Day* books, to find such free, or at any rate, cheap pleasures as Brighton in the summer affords. Mr. Drabble collected their plates and cutlery on a tray and began to wash up. Mrs. Drabble asked John whether he required more toast, and on being told that he had plenty—as indeed she could see; he had only nibbled the corner of one piece—she leaned her back against the sideboard, lit a cigarette, and disposed herself for a good gossip. Funny lot, Americans were, she said. Nice, as a rule, not picky about things like the English, but they did want such odd things, showers and single taps so you could adjust the temperature of the water. Some even went so far as to ask for private bathrooms and television in their rooms. "Think we're the bleeding Pavillion Vista," said Mrs. Drabble indignantly.

John was wondering how he could bring the conversation around to Mrs. Barnes without making it obvious that she was the only subject he wanted to discuss, but Mrs. Drabble took the problem out of his hands. "Mary Barnes still in the B & B lark?" she asked. Drabble, at the sink, gave a short laugh, probably meant to comment on the singular lack of larkishness on the part of Mrs. Barnes.

"No," said John, "Mrs. Barnes works at the theater as a cleaner. So does her husband. He's a very good carpenter and we're lucky to have him."

"Cleaner," said Mrs. Drabble. "Yes, that would suit Mary. No one ever was such a fanatic housekeeper. 'I can't sit here drinking tea all day, Mrs. Drabble,' she used to say to me. 'I've the lodgers' beds to do and the lounge to turn out.' 'Just give it a lick and a promise,' I used to tell her. 'You'll only have to do it again tomorrow.' " She poured herself a cup of stewed tea from a pot by the sink, and sat down at the table next to John's. He offered her a cigarette, hoping she would go on about Mrs. Barnes without having to be prompted.

"Barnes was a good sort," said Mrs. Drabble, inhaling deeply. "Ta. Mrs. B. didn't like it when he and Drabble went round to the pub together. Very strict with him she was."

Drabble nodded and poured himself some tea, looking very willing to join the gossip about the Barneses, but Mrs. Drabble said, "You'd better get on with the beds, Drabble. He'd stand about talking all day, Drabble would," she said after her husband, hastily gulping his tea, had left the room. "You should have seen him and Barnes sometimes when they'd got a bit cheerful at the pub. It didn't happen often, because Barnes was afraid of Mary, but every now and then, well, you can't spend your whole life in chapel, I always say. It was a real treat hearing Barnes come home, singing at the top of his voice. A very nice voice Barnes had. Of course Mrs. B.'d be waiting up for him at the door with a rolling pin in her hand, I shouldn't wonder. I *would* have liked to be a fly on the wall, I used to tell Drabble, to hear what she'd got to say to him. Because she never let on to us, you know. I'd pop in for elevenses the next morning and you'd think nothing had happened the night before. That was Mary Barnes for you. She minded more about appearances than anybody I ever met."

"Barnes keeps very sober these days," said John to keep her going.

"Does he now? Well, I can't say I'm surprised. Mary Barnes always got her way. Always but once."

"And what was that?"

"A baby. She wanted a baby more than anything in the world. Always in and out of doctors' offices they were, she and Barnes. There wasn't nothing they wouldn't try. Taking her temperature every morning, even surgery once, but nothing worked. Her tubes were in a shocking state."

"Why not adopt?" asked John, to head her off from Mary Barnes's tubes.

"There! Just what I used to say to her. If I had a pound for every time I said, 'Why not adopt, Mrs. Barnes,' I'd be a lady of leisure this very moment, living on the Costa Brava, you can take my word for it, Mr. Silk. But no, she wouldn't consider it. 'You don't know where they come from,' she used to tell me. 'Why, supposing the father was a criminal, or the mother a bad woman . . .' A great believer in heredity she was. 'More likely a nice girl what's got herself in trouble,' I used to say. 'Nice girls don't get into trouble,' she said to me." Mrs. Drabble punctuated this statement with a derisive hoot. " 'Maybe not up in Yorkshire, where you come from,' I told her, 'but you can take my word for it, everywhere else in the world nice girls get in trouble every day of the week.' "

John wondered whether Mrs. Drabble's view of the world was perhaps a little lurid, or whether the young people of Rigby were really unusually sedate. True, there was the occasional hasty marriage, the seven-months baby which miraculously weighed eight and a half pounds, but a town whose main claim to scandal was an alderman who'd got a Pierrot dancer at Scarborough pier pregnant in 1951 hardly bore out Mrs. Drabble's dire notion of nice girls. What an old-fashioned expression it was, come to think of it. The pill, he supposed, had erased the very concept of "nice girl," meaning one who saved herself—another antiquated idea—for marriage. Except Verity Barnes, of course. Verity might be an endangered species, but in the true Victorian sense of the word, Verity was a nice girl.

"Did you know Verity?" he asked.

"Ho! Who didn't know Verity. The sun rose and set on that baby. There never was another baby in the world before Verity, or since, to hear Mrs. Barnes tell it. Still, I will say, she was a very nice baby."

"She is a very nice young woman," said John, who was growing tired of the stuffy breakfast room. He looked at the clock on the wall, and seeing that it was past eleven, suggested to Mrs. Drabble that they might go round to the pub for a drink. She bridled at first, but even as she said she didn't know, she was sure, she was pulling the curlers from her hair and untying the pink plastic apron she wore to serve breakfast.

After the subterranean breakfast room, John was startled by the brilliance of the day. The sun shone from a deep blue sky, the water sparkled so brightly it hurt the eye. Children screeched as curly waves fringed with white foam slid over their bare feet. Up and down the Front people congratulated each other on the fine day.

Thinking that Mrs. Drabble would enjoy something la-de-da, he suggested the bar of one of the hotels along the Front, but she opted for her usual local, wanting to be seen, by envious neighbors, in the society of so distinguished a gentleman.

His face courteously hiding his feelings about port and lime, John ordered a large one for Mrs. Drabble and a small dry sherry for himself. After they had tasted their drinks, John, as if there had been no interruption in their talk, said, "Yes, Verity is a very nice girl. And the Barneses still dote on her. It's good to know Mrs. Barnes's efforts were finally so well rewarded."

"Bless you, Mary Barnes didn't *have* her," said Mrs. Drabble, finishing off her port and lime. "I told you, she couldn't, try however she might. Why, her tubes . . ." John signalled the barmaid for another drink for Mrs. Drabble, but he was not to be spared a guided tour of the Barnes interior. Mrs. Drabble, like many uneducated women, took a passionate interest in things obstetrical, and spared him not the smallest detail of Mary Barnes's reproductive system. He abstracted his mind till she should have talked herself to a standstill, then, ordering her another drink, said, "But you told me she wouldn't adopt. Did she change her mind?"

Mrs. Drabble accepted her third port and lime in an absent manner, as if she had not noticed the repeated change of glasses and was under the impression that she was still sipping her first.

"Well, she must have, mustn't she," she said, referring to Mrs. Barnes's change of mind. "But, you know, Mr. Silk, I don't think it was a regular adoption. There weren't any people from the adoption agency snooping about asking the neighbors if she'd be a good mother, you know the way they do. Unless that man . . . Funny, I haven't thought of him from that day to this."

"A man?" asked John. Mrs. Drabble sat gazing into the distance for so long that he wondered whether he had been too generous with the drinks. But she returned to earth suddenly, took a refined sip from her glass and said, "There now, isn't it funny, I never put two and two together. And Drabble and I talked of it night after night, it was so strange. I mean Mary Barnes going off for two days and coming back with a new baby. 'Why, Mrs. Barnes, you've been and done it after all,' I said to her, meaning adopted."

" 'Hardly, Mrs. Drabble,' she said as if I'd meant it was her own. And her as flat as an ironing board. She'd get a look on her face sometimes when she was put out, like the Queen when she declares Parliament open, if you know what I mean." John, who had encountered the look several times, said he did indeed. " 'It's my sister's child,' she said with her Queen Elizabeth look. 'My sister has never been strong, and she was very pulled down by the birth, so I'm going to look after the baby for now. She's a little girl called Verity, and Barnes and I are delighted to have her.' Well, it's possible, I'm not saying it isn't. All I know is that was the first time I ever heard of a sister, so I just never quite believed it."

Her glass was empty. John signalled the barmaid once again. "What had it to do with the man?" he asked.

"What man?"

"The one you said . . ."

"Oh, him. Well, it was funny. Ordinarily I wouldn't have made anything of it, but it was just a week before Mrs. Barnes turned up with Verity, so it does make you think."

"Perhaps he simply wanted to rent a room," said John,

wondering whether Mrs. Drabble was merely trying to add mystery to what was not, after all, a very exciting story, or whether the man really had something to do with Verity.

"No, he didn't, that I do know," said Mrs. Drabble firmly. "I was pegging out the washing when he rang the bell at the Wellington, and when there was no answer I called to him and told him Mrs. Barnes had gone out to do her shopping. We still used to stand on queues then if you'll remember, Mr. Silk, and sometimes it took half a day just to get a meal together, especially when it was Mary Barnes. Everything had to be just so, or she'd argue with the shopkeepers till she had her way. I told him she wouldn't be long though. I knew she'd be getting Barnes's dinner at twelve, and she was always on the dot with meals." The word "dinner" seemed to remind her of her own duties. She glanced at the clock and began to gather up her bag. "Lord, I'd no idea," she said. "Drabble will be wondering what happened to his dinner."

"Just one more," John said, wanting to hear the end of the story. Mrs. Drabble, conceding that a bird couldn't fly on one wing, accepted her fifth port and lime, while John took the second sip of his small sherry.

"What happened about the man," he asked.

"Oh, him? He said he'd be back in the afternoon, and would I tell Mrs. Barnes a Mr. Ryan had called. I said was he looking for a room, happening to know the Wellington was full up, but he said no, it was something personal. 'Well,' I said to him, 'if you're a commercial I wish you luck. The Rock of Gibraltar is softer than Mrs. B.'s heart when it comes to door-to-doors. Yorkshire, you know.' He laughed at that and said, 'I'm Yorkshire myself,' and just then Mary Barnes came around the corner, and, believe me, Mr. Silk, if looks could kill I'd be in my grave these eighteen years." She finished up the last of her drink and gathered up her purse. "Funny, isn't it? I've thought of the Barneses and Verity many a time, but I'd forgotten all about him. Anyhow, a week later Mary Barnes came home with the baby and a month later the Wellington was up for sale. She wanted to go back to Yorkshire, she said. The South was no place to bring up a child. 'Well, we were all brought up here, and we survived,' I told her. But Joe Stayling couldn't change Mary Barnes with her mind made up, and within two months they were gone. We exchanged Christmas cards the first few years, but I haven't heard from her for a long time."

The brilliant day had clouded over while they had sat in the pub, and a chill wind blew in from the sea. John saw Mrs. Drabble back to the Shangri La, and then went to the English Oyster Bar, to lunch temperately but well on half a dozen Colchester oysters. As he slowly savored each sparkling mollusc he thought about the tale Mrs. Drabble had told him and, try as he might, could not find in it any connection with Ally. It was most unlikely that he should have had anything to do with the begetting of Verity, this not being Ally's line. Even if such an incongruous event had taken place, it was hardly a motive for murder. John took a lighthearted view of illegitimacy, being himself the haphazard result of the 1918 armistice celebrations. Though he realized that certain people, Mrs. Barnes undoubtedly among them, might look upon bastardy more severely than he did himself, he could not imagine that it would, in this day and age, cause anyone to kill to keep it secret. Yet something about the story stuck in his mind, something which had, as Mrs. Drabble talked with horrid fluency, tapped his mind for admission, but had tapped so gently that it had not been taken notice of. It was not likely to be important, thought John, since Mrs. Drabble's story, while entertaining enough, could not by any stretch of the imagination be brought to bear on Ally's murder.

And yet . . . What had Verity meant when she had said to her mother, "You know why I'm going to keep seeing Tim, and you know why you can't stop me"? Over a cup of indifferent coffee, he rehearsed various readings of this line in his head. Had she meant, "I'll keep on seeing him because

I'm in love with him, and you can't stop me because I'm eighteen, earning my own living, and if you get too interfering I'll find a place of my own to live"? He could imagine a good many daughters speaking like this to their mothers, but it was not how Verity had ever before spoken to Mrs. Barnes. Yet it was even less likely that she had meant, "You killed his lover, and if you try to interfere I'll tell the police."

Having spent his life in the theater, John was more familiar with the houses of Atreus and Lear than the lives of an average English family. Judging by the plays of the Angry Young Men, all was not as serene on the home front as the cozy afternoon tea, corpse-on-the-library-floor plays of his youth had pretended. He wished he had been present to hear Verity actually saying those words to her mother, to hear the tone of voice, the amount of anger behind the words. For, read them as he might, he could not imagine himself directing an actress of Verity's type to speak this line with any conviction or verisimilitude.

Ah well, he would tell Inspector Winterkill what he knew and leave it to the police to sort it out. He settled his account and for the rest of the afternoon allowed himself to be gently amused by the extravagant architecture of the Pavillion, and the comments of the American tourists.

Generally speaking, Barnes held few opinions about actors. He liked John Silk, who always treated him courteously, as well he might, seeing how little he could afford to pay, and heartily disliked the stuck-up ones—Nell Wood and Bertie de Grey. On Verity's account he disliked and distrusted Tim Selkirk, but the others blurred into a background of people who came and went, making it hardly worth his while to know their names.

This summer there was one exception. Gavin Beauclerc, who had carried over into adult life a boyhood passion for carpentry, had taken to hanging about the tidy little shed behind the theater to watch Barnes at work. The lad would never amount to more than an amateur, in Barnes's opinion. He hadn't the time to give to it, what with rehearsals and matinees and such. Why anyone would want to stand on a stage wearing funny clothes, talking rubbish written by someone else when he might have spent his days working with wood, Barnes could not imagine. "Daft," was his brief judgment of such behavior, but few people can resist the flattery of discipleship, and this very afternoon Barnes had promised to show Gavin how to dovetail; the skill which separates the true carpenter from the botcher. He was at work on a replica of a Regency secretary for a future production of *The Rivals,* and while many a stage carpenter would have felt that for a prop a bit of glue was good enough, especially on the inside, where it didn't show, that was not Barnes's way. While he waited for Gavin he set out his dovetail saw and got ready the pieces of wood to be fitted for the drawer. He tested the saw with his thumb, delighting in the feel of the blade. There were carpenters, Barnes knew, who used a high-speed electric router for dovetailing, but people like that were only fit to work in a furniture factory, so far as Barnes was concerned. By the time Gavin came in, full of apologies for being late—it was his fault entirely, he said, he'd been fluffing his lines all day—everything was ready.

In his slow and circumstantial way Barnes explained what he was going to do but, when he picked up the saw, Gavin could hardly follow its movements, so quickly did it bite into the wood and turn the corners.

"There we are then," said Barnes, in what seemed to Gavin an incredibly short time. He held up the two pieces of wood, with their tails and pins neatly cut out. Gavin, who had often tried this trick without once succeeding in fitting the finished pieces together, held his breath as the tails and pins slid into place, fitting as neatly as a jigsaw puzzle.

"Fantastic," said Gavin. "It's like a magic trick when you do it. I've tried, but nothing ever quite fits."

"There's some wood here, if you'd like to have a go," said

Barnes, embarrassed but not displeased by such openly expressed admiration. He gave Gavin two pieces of scrap wood and showed him what to do. Then, realizing that the lad would be all thumbs with a master craftsman watching over his shoulder, he kindly turned away, took up a broom and began to sweep a mound of wood shavings and sawdust into a plastic bag.

"It's for my garden," he explained, while the dovetail saw, sounding uncertain and hesitant, made its way around the notches Barnes had drawn on the wood. "It's a fine mulch, wood is, so long as you remember to put it on top of a layer of manure. Eat all your nitrogen, wood does, and your plants starve to death if you forget the muck. Why, whatever is that?" He stopped sweeping up the sawdust and stood looking at a brown paper bag, from which protruded the head of a bottle.

Gavin, not sorry to be able to stop what was not going to be a successful dovetail, said, "What's the matter, what is it?"

"A bottle it looks like," said Barnes, sliding it from its bag. "Gin! Oo's been 'iding 'is drink in my shop?" he said, his indignation scattering the h's, which Mrs. Barnes had worked hard to put there, from his speech. "Get me in trouble with t'missus, this would . . ." His voice faded as the realization hit him.

The word BOMBAY formed a canopy of ornate lettering above the plump, stern face of Queen Victoria. "It's Ally's," said Gavin, his voice hoarse. He cleared his throat. "It must be. It's the poisoned gin."

"Oh cripes, I shouldn't have touched it," said Barnes. "But 'ow was I supposed to know?" He cautiously slid the bottle back into its bag and put it back on the floor where he had found it under the sawdust, handling it as gingerly as if it contained nitroglycerine instead of gin. "Well, lad," he said, "you'd better go and phone for the police. I'll stay here and see nobody monkeys with it."

When John returned to the Shangri La, two telephone messages awaited him, one bogus, called in by himself with a French accent, telling him to get in touch with his agent in London at once, the other genuine, from Gavin Beauclerc, asking him to call the theater as soon as possible. Mrs. Drabble lingered in the hall, hoping for drama, but John waited till she at last retreated to the lounge and shut the door. The theater answered promptly, and Gavin told him that Ally's bottle of Bombay gin had been found, hidden under a pile of sawdust in Barnes's carpentry shop, that according to Inspector Winterkill it contained a small amount of gin, and an as yet unspecified amount of rat poison. Its outside was marked with the clear fingerprints of Bertie de Grey, who was at this very moment assisting the police in their enquiries.

CHAPTER X

It was Verity's first visit to the Budgie Cage. The blare of the rock band, the strobe lights pulsing through the thick cigarette smoke, the dancers jammed on the small floor, scarcely moving, never touching, made her feel dizzy at first. A waitress in bell-bottom trousers and a see-through top said something to Tim. The music was so loud Verity couldn't hear her, and she was too embarrassed by the transparent shirt to look at her. Tim, inured to noise, ordered a beer for himself and orange squash for Verity. He looked around the smoky room, so unexpected, he thought, in an out-of-the-way dump like Yorkshire, and shouted, "What a gas. Come on, let's dance."

Verity followed him to the crowded dance floor. She had been worried that she would not know the steps, but quickly realized that there was no need to know anything; you simply stood in one place, snapped your fingers to the rhythm of the band, shuffled your feet and gyrated (if you could bring yourself to do it, which Verity most certainly could not) around your own pelvis. Verity copied the other dancers as much as she could and, never being a great talker, was thankful that the noise of the band made conversation impossible. The band, having worked itself up into a great fury, with the singers howling like damned souls and beating their guitars with their fists, yelling, "Yeah, yeah, yeah," suddenly ceased its frenzy and was still. The silence beat on Verity's ears. The band was apparently not very popular with the cognoscenti of the Budgie Cage, for the applause was scattered and the band's want of funk was earnestly discussed by the more musical members of the audience.

The room was very hot. Verity drank her orange squash, wishing the glass and the table were not so sticky. The room was too dark to show up dirt, but Verity suspected that in daylight everything would look very grimy indeed. She decided not to drink any more of her squash, so that she would not be forced to use the ladies' room. It was very exciting, being in the Budgie Cage, a place which had been preached against in chapel as a Yorkshire Whore of Babylon, but she was not entirely sure that she was having fun. She had had to lie to her mother to be allowed to stay out so late, and this weighed on her conscience. She was relieved when the band began to play again. They could dance now, and she would no longer have to think.

At a corner table she saw Inspector Winterkill sitting by himself, looking tired and bored. Beryl, her marvelous palomino tail of hair nearly touching the hem of her miniskirt, danced with a much younger man. Verity felt very sorry for the inspector, though she knew that it had been wrong of him to divorce Mavis Winterkill and marry a young woman.

The band played on and on, and the longer she danced, the happier Verity felt. Tim, entirely absorbed in the motions of his body and the pounding of the music, smiled to himself and seemed unaware of her. At the end of the set the band began to play something slow, romantic and sad; the Beatles' "Golden Slumbers." Couples moved together and danced slowly, closely embraced. "Once there was a way to get back homeward," the lead singer sang, and Verity, dancing in a nightclub with a young man her parents disapproved of, felt a pleasant melancholy as she thought that she was growing away from her happy childhood and the safety of home. Then Tim's body pressed against hers, and she forgot her sadness, feeling only the warm tingling shiver on her skin, as Tim drew her closer and closer. Before coming to the club they had parked to look at the moon shining down on the ruined castle, and Verity, rather nervous of the Budgie Cage, had allowed Tim longer innings than usual, so that he had come very close to getting past third base and scoring. Now, dancing slowly and sensuously, amid a crowd of other couples just as closely pressed together, Verity felt exactly as she had in the car just before she had summoned all the strength of her Rigby upbringing to her aid and had gasped a breathless, "Stop!" Inspector Winterkill and Beryl danced past her, but she was not aware of them. When the music at last ended and Verity went with Tim back to their table, she felt as weak at the knees as if she had just had a terrible fright. Tim, no fool in such matters, ordered another beer for himself, and said to her, "Why don't you have a real drink, Verity, instead of that sticky kid stuff?" Verity thought this over, and perhaps affected by breathing the smoke of the crowded room which came by no means entirely from legal cigarettes, asked, "What was it Mr. Jagat used to drink?"

"Martinis," said Tim. "Gin, and a drop of vermouth." He thought it a splendid choice. On a girl like Verity, unused to any kind of drink, gin might be expected to have magical effects. "A gin and French for the lady," he said to the waitress, having learned from Ally that if you order a martini in England you get something else. He and Verity held hands while they waited for their drinks. The band had begun to play again. A red light circled the room, the strobe lights pulsed blue and green, the music pounded with the steady rhythm of a beating heart. Tim lit a joint, and Verity accepted a puff. She had tried smoking several times before, feeling very sophisticated and sinful, but the smoke had only caused her to cough, and she had never experienced the loosening of thought and sinew which overcame her this time. "I think I'm tiddley," she said with a giggle.

"You haven't had your drink yet," said Tim, handing her the joint again. The waitress arrived and put down his beer and Verity's martini. Tim drank thirstily, but Verity picked up her glass with some anxiety.

"Do you really think I should?" she asked, losing her nerve and putting the glass back on the table.

"Sure you should," Tim said encouragingly. "Like, you know, why not?"

Verity picked up the glass and sniffed it like a suspicious animal. She looked at Tim, puzzled at first and then afraid.

"What's the matter?" he asked. "Is it lousy?" She did not seem to have heard him. "What's the matter?" he asked again.

Cautiously, as if the glass might explode, she sniffed once more. "That's not it," she said.

"It's not what? What's the matter, Verity?"

"It's not what Mr. Jagat drank."

Tim picked up the glass and took a sip. "Sure it is," he said. "Like, they probably watered it down some, but it's a martini all right."

Verity dumbly shook her head. "It isn't. It can't be."

"Look," said Tim, "if you don't like it, don't drink it, okay? What do you say we get out of here," he added, wanting to get her inside Mick's car so they could park and look at the moon some more. But Verity had dropped her face into her hands and was sobbing, "Oh no, it can't be," over and over. Tim, baffled and annoyed, wondered what had caused this peculiar reaction. She'd only had two drags off his joint, and she never inhaled anyhow, so she could hardly have had a bad reaction from the pot. And she'd done no more than sniff the martini. Then what the hell . . .

Inspector Winterkill and Beryl, on their way out, stopped by their table. "What's the matter, Verity, are you feeling ill?" the inspector asked.

"It's awfully close in here," said Beryl sympathetically. "Why don't you come outside and get a breath of air, luv?"

Verity, passive as a rag doll, allowed Beryl to put her jacket over her shoulders and lead her outside. The inspector picked up Verity's glass and tasted the martini. "Seems all right," he said. "But you should know better than to let

Verity drink gin, Selkirk. She's not used to drink. Mind you take her straight home now. No parking and snogging on the way, understand?" Tim wanted to ask what business of his it was, but remembering the cash advance and airline ticket he had charged on his mother's card, as well as the sixty-five pounds he had kept back from Ally's money, he meekly said he would.

Outside, in the cool, fresh air, Verity had pulled herself together sufficiently to thank Beryl and assure the inspector that she was all right. But in the car she began to sniffle again, so that Tim, cross with her for wasting his evening, found it easy enough to obey Inspector Winterkill's order and take her directly home without any parking, or—as the inspector had so quaintly put it—"snogging," on the way.

"Johnny," said Bertie de Grey, "you must get in touch with Amnesty International at once. I am being tortured."

The young policeman who had escorted John Silk into the visitors' room, looked over their heads, pretending to take no interest in what was said, but his ears grew noticeably pink. Bertie de Grey had done nothing to endear himself to the constabulary, having been both supercilious and unhelpful. His questioning had been lengthy and rigorous in consequence. With his white stubble of unshaven beard, dishevelled hair and bloodshot eyes, he looked far more like a derelict brought in from the gutter to sleep it off than a once famous actor. But since there were no marks of violence on him, John took the accusation as part of Bertie's customary hyperbole. He said, "You look a bit draggled, but hardly like someone who's undergone the third degree, Bertie."

"Ha!" said Bertie, striking a pose so dramatic that the young constable, though still pretending to take no notice, could not quite hide his grin. "There is such a thing as psychological torture. Did you bring me a drink, Johnny?"

"I did."

"Oh, bless you."

"Unfortunately they confiscated it at the desk."

"There, what did I tell you. They are probably guzzling it at this very moment."

"They are not. They said I could have it back when I leave. I shall save it and bring it with me when they let you out of here."

"When indeed. What, I ask you, has become of the law of *habeas corpus?* I am being held incommunicado, my dear, like some poor dago by a goon squad in a banana republic. It's intolerable."

"Poor Bertie. Why wouldn't you see a lawyer?"

"Lawyers!" said Bertie with the utmost contempt. "You seem to forget that I enjoyed a phenomenal run in *Bleak House.* There is very little I don't know about lawyers and their ways. Greedy shysters who take your money and do nothing for it. I am an innocent man, I don't need a lawyer. I need a drink and something to eat."

"Inspector Winterkill says you threw the breakfast tray at Constable Harding's head."

"It wasn't breakfast, it was swill."

"I expect it was a very nice breakfast."

"India tea!"

"Bertie, do be reasonable. Let me ring up your solicitor. And tell the police what they want to know."

"I have no solicitor. I need no solicitor. I am perfectly capable of spending the pittance you pay me without the help of a solicitor. And as for telling them what they want to know, haven't I confessed to every murder from Cain to Long Liz Stride."

"Who on earth was Long Liz Stride?"

"Honestly, Johnny, how uneducated."

"She was one of Jack the Ripper's young ladies, sir," said the constable, putting it delicately.

"I'll ask Burke to come and see you," said John. "He does the legal work for the theater, and he's very competent.

He'll be able to advise you. And my dear," John put his hand over the old man's, "please don't throw any more trays, and do answer their questions properly. I want you out of here, back at the theater where you belong."

The wrinkled, clammy hand under his trembled. All the grand airs and superiority suddenly went out of Bertie. He slumped over the table. "Oh Christ, Johnny, what can I tell them. My fingerprints are on the bottle and there was poison in the gin."

"Your fingerprints could have been on that bottle for any number of reasons. Perhaps you picked it up and moved it, or you might have taken a nip of it and forgotten."

Bertie looked a trifle shifty at this. "Well," he said, "I did, as a matter of fact, happen to take a tiny nip after Ally had gone on stage. Ally wouldn't have minded. He wasn't one to grudge a friend a drop of gin."

"Of course not. Tell the police, Bertie."

"I did. They didn't believe me. They wanted to know why, in that case, I wasn't dead. And Johnny, I've no explanation for that."

"Talk with Burke," said John soothingly. "He'll be able to advise you what to do."

"There's nothing to do. Nothing." The old man rubbed the back of his hand across his nose. John gave him a clean handkerchief, barely able to look at the stubbly face, suddenly so defeated. He hated to see anyone brought low, but hated it most of all in an old man who had nothing left but his imperious manner.

The young constable looked at his watch in the way of one who expects to be seen doing it. "I think they want me to leave," said John. "Please, Bertie, promise me to talk to Burke."

"What was it?" Bertie de Grey asked.

"What was what?"

"The drink you brought me. What kind was it?"

"Your favorite. Beefeaters."

"Oh Christ!" The head, with its aureole of white tangled hair, slumped on the table. "Oh Christ," he sobbed, "I wish you hadn't told me."

"I don't believe it," said John. "Not any of it."

"What don't you believe?"

"That Bertie de Grey killed Ally. Or that you think so."

Inspector Winterkill looked at John with the air of someone who is trying to be patient with a not-very-bright child. "His fingerprints were on that bottle."

"Carefully preserved and wrapped in a paper bag to make sure the police would find them. Inspector, you are talking about a man who had a three-year West End run playing Sherlock Holmes."

"In my experience actors can be remarkably silly where practical matters are concerned."

"I'm told the bottle was found in Barnes's carpentry shop," said John, unwilling to discuss the excessive silliness of actors when confronted by real life.

"That's right," said the inspector stolidly.

"But surely the carpentry shop was searched by the police the night of the murder. They would hardly have overlooked as sizeable an object as a bottle."

"If you ask me, Gaskell and Troutt could overlook the Rock of Gibraltar."

"Bertie says he took a swig of gin after Ally went on stage. This seems both plausible and in character. That he should poison the gin, leave his fingerprints on the bottle, wrap it in a brown paper bag so they shouldn't get smudged, and hide it in Barnes's shed, where it was bound to get found sooner or later is, even for someone as eccentric as Bertie de Grey, a little hard to swallow."

"Then how do you explain that after he took that swig he claims to have taken, he showed no signs whatever of having swallowed rat poison?"

"I don't for a moment believe the gin in the bottle was

poisoned. Have you had a report on it yet? I mean, was the proportion of rat poison to gin the same as that which was in the drink Ally swallowed?"

The inspector, who had told County Forensic that there was no hurry, said, "Not yet. But I expect it'll match."

"You wouldn't care to put money on that, would you? May I tell you what I think?" John took a cigarette from the packet that the inspector slid across the table. "I think," he said, "that the murderer saw Bertie take a drink that night and knew his prints were on the bottle. In the mix-up after the murder this person hid the bottle in case it should be needed later on. Until now the murderer hasn't felt threatened. Now suddenly he does and allows the bottle to be found, thus considerably widening the field of people who might have poisoned Ally's gin."

"That's very neat," said the inspector. "I'd rather hoped it wouldn't have occurred to you. It hasn't yet occurred to the super. Well, nothing ever does unless you write it out in block letters in words of one syllable. So I'm taking advantage of the situation."

"You're taking advantage of a poor old man who has done nothing but be disagreeable."

"Disagreeable! I'll tell you something. Bertie de Grey has raised disagreeableness to an art form. Believe me, having him here is harder on us than it is on him."

John laughed. "What advantage are you hoping to buy at the price of keeping Bertie here?"

"I want to lull the murderer," said the inspector. "I want him, or her, to think he's safe, that we've fallen for the trick. I'm hoping that with Bertie de Grey sitting in a prison cell the murderer will make a wrong move."

John considered this. "Aren't you doing something that's illegal?"

The inspector shrugged. "Let's say we're stretching the rules."

"I feel very uncomfortable with that."

"It's done every day."

"That makes me more uncomfortable yet. The police are here, after all, to uphold the rules and punish those who break them."

"In theory. In practice—" The inspector shrugged. "Murderers aren't caught by boy scouts, Silk. We have to use the opportunities the gods provide. You want Jagat's murderer to be caught, don't you?"

"Yes, yes, of course I do."

"Well then, let us catch him. Look," he said, seeing that John still looked unhappy, "nobody's being harmed. De Grey isn't really being tortured—we are, if anybody is—we'll do him a favor and dry up his liver a bit in the meantime. The law isn't really being broken, just bent a little, and with any luck someone will make a wrong move."

"Perhaps someone has already. I mean, something must have prompted the murderer to let the bottle be found. What is suddenly making him feel threatened?"

"Your trip to Brighton?"

"I'm afraid not." John told the inspector Mrs. Drabble's story. Inspector Winterkill was not impressed. "I can't see what it could have to do with Jagat," he said. "From what you tell me, it's not likely that Verity's his daughter, and not even Mary Barnes would poison somebody to keep it secret that she's adopted. Not in this day and age." John agreed. "Well, at least you got a day by the sea," the inspector said. "I could do with some time off myself."

Yet something in the story snagged his memory, as it had John's when Mrs. Drabble had told it to him. The inspector was far too experienced a policeman to try and force his mind to remember. "You only block things off that way," he told himself. "Leave it be." It would come while he was half awake, thinking of something else, or in the middle of the night, like the time he had sat bolt upright at three in the morning and said "myxomatosis" because he and Mavis had been trying to remember what it was that had killed off all the rabbits back in the early fifties. Mavis had got a rare laugh out of that one.

Yet he had to tell himself repeatedly to stop worrying at the memory. Something like the first tickle in the nose warning of a sneeze coming on, a sense that whatever it was he couldn't remember was important, might even be the key which would unlock the entire case, nagged at him all that afternoon. He couldn't leave it alone. Ah well, he thought, getting ready to go home to dinner, Beryl's cooking would put it right out of his mind, with the pangs of indigestion taking its place.

CHAPTER XI

Tim Selkirk sat outside the airplane spotting shelter, waiting for Verity Barnes. The day, though sunny and still, held a small warning of autumn chill. The dales rolled away at Tim's feet like gigantic breakers of purple heather. Though their motion was away from him, they seemed to be crowding nearer in the glassy air, almost as if they were stealthily walking toward him. He felt a sense of panic in the shimmer of the sun. Beautiful as they were, the dales could be frightening too, not so much on days of howling wind and black skies, but on days like this, of clear sun and a capacious silence.

"Deserts of vast eternity." The line came back to him as it had many times since his talk with John Silk. If that was what poetry did to you, stick in your mind like the burrs which clung to his jeans, he wanted no part of it. The fact was that Tim was in a bad mood, and nothing pleased him since a tear-sodden Verity had grasped his arm last evening and pulled him into the prop room to tell him, her speech rendered almost incomprehensible with sobs, that her father had absolutely, once and for all, forbidden her to see Tim Selkirk ever again.

She had been away from the theater for three days after their visit to the Budgie Cage; ill, it was said, though no specific ailment was mentioned. When Tim got up the courage to ask Mr. Barnes, whom he found slightly more accessible than Mrs. Barnes, whether Verity was all right, he got a surly, "No thanks to you, lad," for answer.

Even when she had come back to the theater she had avoided him. Whenever he saw her, there seemed to be one of her parents nearby, watching. At last, between a matinee and the evening performance, both Barneses were busy elsewhere and Verity seized her chance.

"But why?" said Tim. "We didn't do anything wrong."

"We went to the Budgie Cage."

"You didn't have to tell them."

"Oh," she said, sobbing, "you don't understand what they're like."

In fact Verity, unlike most of her contemporaries, was unaccustomed to fighting with her parents. Never before had her father spoken to her as he had that night, calling her a liar and a trollop, while her mother had sat silent and dry-eyed, like the Greek lady Verity had read about in school, who had been turned to stone by grief. Long after Verity had been sent to bed, Mrs. Barnes came up the stairs and quietly opened her door. Verity, who had been staring wide-eyed into the dark, closed her eyes, pretending to be asleep. There was a small clink on the night table, then soft steps, and the door was once again closed. Verity lit her bedside lamp and saw that her mother had left her a glass of hot milk. She drank it obediently, was promptly sick, and finally wept herself to sleep.

Tim felt nothing but irritation. Tears did not become Verity. Her pretty face looked spongy and splotched. Her red eyes reminded Tim of an albino rabbit he had let die of neglect when his first boyish interest in the curious creature had waned.

"What does he think, that we had it off in the Budgie Cage?" he said crudely.

"Oh Tim, don't."

"Oh Tim don't what?"

"Talk like that."

The reminder that he had in fact not had it off, came at an unfortunate time. Already cross with the soggy girl who hadn't enough backbone to stand up to that ridiculous little father of hers, it made him doubly cross to be reminded of his failure to succeed with her. His patience with her many scruples, all of which were as meaningless to him as a religious rite practiced by a Zulu, was not to be rewarded, it seemed, with the prize of Verity's virginity, and all because her idiotic father had to act like somebody in a Victorian melodrama and forbid her to see him.

Though he no longer wanted her, at least not at that moment, he nevertheless decided to have her, like a quarrelsome person insisting on the last word. He felt as he had sometimes when, having camped on the sidewalk all night to get tickets for a rock concert, the box-office window was slammed down and the SOLD OUT notice put up before he could reach it.

Once again he trotted out the only weapon which, his winning looks aside, he possessed. "Well, I guess I might as well go back to London in that case," he said.

As a threat it had never before worked, partly because Verity had not entirely believed it. But now, as she looked at him, his blue eyes hard with annoyance, the droop of self-pity at the corner of his mouth, the threat was suddenly real, and Verity, infatuated and frightened, gave a great sob of anguish. Tim, loathing her sodden, swollen face, put an arm around her to hide it against his buckskin jacket.

Gradually her sobs quieted. Tim, thinking as clearly as his annoyance with her allowed, had arrived at a decision. Just as the tickets to rock concerts past had increased in desirability as they had become unavailable—so that he had on occasion paid outrageous sums of money or given away a precious horde of purple owsleys to attend a concert he had only mildly wanted to hear—so now Verity, at her most unattractive, tear-slobbered and sniffling worst, became an object he had to have before he went away.

He lifted her damp face, kissed her very gently and then took her in his arms, murmuring inarticulate endearments.

"There," he finally said, as she fetched up a deep and final sigh and, finding her handkerchief, began to mop her eyes.

He said, "Listen, Verity, it's like, we can't say goodbye in this dump. Somebody might come in any minute. Do just one thing for me, okay? Meet me once more up, you know, by our usual place. Tomorrow afternoon, just, like, to say goodbye properly. Okay?"

It was not a bad speech for someone who had no practice in such matters, he and his former female companions having drifted together and separated as inarticulately and passively as amoeba. Verity, accustomed in her working life to the high rhetoric of leave-taking suitable to Romeo and Anthony, was as lacking in personal experience as Tim, though for different reasons. He was no Romeo, but he moved her enough to agree to defy her father, who, for the first time in her life, had truly frightened her.

"I'll have to tell Dad," she said. "He keeps me locked in my room except for coming to meals and going to work. But I'll tell him it's the last time, just to say goodbye. I know he'll understand."

She was so young she had very nearly recovered her looks in the short time it had taken to talk, and Tim kissed her with a return of genuine affection and desire.

Up by the spotters' shelter a cool breeze had sprung up, and Tim shivered a little. His watch, an expensive and handsome gift from Ally, had never kept time well, but the sun was low in the sky and the air had grown chilly. Out of a farmer's field hundreds of pigeons took flight. The air was so silent he could hear the sound of their wings, like paper being rustled by a wind. Was Verity not coming after all? She was such a punctual girl usually; it was far more often that he had kept her waiting. He looked down the field path which led up from the village, but a curve of hill hid it for most of the way.

Birds flicked in the sky, returning to their nests. Had Verity changed her mind? Had her father refused to unlock her door? Or had she had second thoughts and decided not to come? Once again he looked at his watch; it told him two-thirty, which was ridiculous. He decided to wait only a very little time longer. The dales, the clear air, the endless solitude made him uneasy. Or was it his thoughts—what Ally's generation might have called his "conscience"?

He was here, waiting to take something from Verity which had no meaning for him but held great value for her. There was a book he had been supposed to read for one of his college courses—he had made do with *Cliff Notes*—about an English servant girl who had spent what seemed like thousands of pages protecting her virginity from the wiles of her employer, whom she reduced to such blithering idiocy that he finally married her. The English were a bunch of weirdos and no mistake. Yet, if it meant so much to her—Verity, not Pamela—maybe he should just leave her alone. Like, what was it to him? It didn't really matter, did it. Anyway, the bomb was going to get them all in the end, him and Rigby and Verity and Verity's virginity. Some day soon there were going to be missiles streaking across the sky, looking far-out and weirdly beautiful, and there would be a burst of light brighter than anyone could imagine, and then the hot, stormy dark.

It was the last thing he was conscious of—the blinding flash of light—then darkness, no pain, no astonishment, and soon, nothing at all.

"There now," said Mrs. Troutt to her son, "he's done a bunk."

Constable Troutt looked into the room with its half-packed duffel bag. Clothes lay tangled on the bed. Four pairs of Frye boots stood in a row.

"Perhaps he's with that pal of his, Mick what's-'is-name from the theater."

"Don't think so, somehow," said Mrs. Troutt, who often rented to actors and was accustomed to sudden departures.

"He owes two weeks' rent. I told him he'd have to pay up or leave."

"Well, those boots ought to fetch something," said the constable, eyeing them regretfully. He'd have loved to keep a pair, but his solid, wide policeman's feet would never squeeze into that slim last. "And that case."

The case was a Vuitton Tim had borrowed from his mother without going through the formality of asking her permission.

"Ugly things, those Whittons," said Mrs. Troutt. "Never could understand why anybody'd pay good money for them."

Her son picked up one of Tim's ruffled shirts. "Nice," he said, "for a girl. You'd look smashing in one of those, Mum."

Mrs. Troutt's ample bosom shook like a jelly when she laughed. "Get on with you," she said, immensely flattered.

"I'll take the whole lot into Scarborough for you," the constable offered. "See what Uncle'll give us."

While attending to this, he dropped in on Inspector Winterkill and told him that Tim Selkirk would seem to have left town owing two weeks' rent. The inspector notified the London police, but Tim had never been a serious suspect, and aside from asking Commander Selkirk to notify them if the young man turned up, no steps were taken to retrieve him.

Inspector Winterkill had been kept busy with a case of pigeon thieving and the ensuing physical mayhem the victimized members of the pigeon fanciers' club inflicted on the suspected perpetrators. Yet, despite the imaginative alibis of one side, and the heartrending tales of loss and despair on the other, the niggling feeling that something in John Silk's Brighton account should have rung a bell, persisted. He told himself over and over not to worry at it lest it should go away entirely, steeped himself in pigeon lore (far more interesting than he would have supposed) and was finally able to arrest the true thieves—a very nasty lot from Redcar—and arrange a tentative peace between the victims and the abused innocent suspects. But through it all, John Silk's story—Mrs. Drabble's story—ran in the back of his mind, not to be silenced, refusing to go away, yet unwilling to yield the nugget of information contained somewhere within.

"Leave it be, it'll come to you while you're asleep," he assured himself last thing every night; and, "Don't worry it, it'll turn up while you're thinking of something else," he warned himself first thing every morning. Just when he had lost hope, and told himself that if it had been important he would have recalled it by now, memory yielded its piece of information—not while he slept, nor while he was thinking of something else, but mischievously, at a time when he was quite beyond thinking at all, right in the middle of one of Beryl's exhilarating quickies.

"Ryan, you chump," said memory, and "Ryan," the inspector said out loud. "Ryan!" The name rendered him incapable of attending to Beryl any further. "Sorry, luv," he said, in such a hurry to put on his clothes and get to the office that he scarcely took note of an inability which would at any other time have plunged him into despondency and self-doubt.

Beryl, amazed and instantly suspicious, accused him of having a new girlfriend (the said Ms. "Ryan," no doubt) and threatened to find her and claw her face to shreds. This was very flattering to a man who would never see forty or his toes again, but the inspector was too preoccupied to take the time to relish Beryl's jealousy.

"Ryan happens to be a man," he said, and kissed her goodbye as absentmindedly as he used to kiss Mavis, hardly noticing what he was doing. A chastened Beryl asked him whether he wouldn't like some breakfast. Since she had never offered to make him so much as a cup of tea before, a less preoccupied man might have been pleased by such a spirit of amendment. But Inspector Winterkill, his mind on

Somerset House, said absently, "Haven't got time, luv. Ta, though." At the door he turned and said, "It was the gin, you see. The gin explains it all," a remark which left Beryl both befuddled and apprehensive.

At his office he waited impatiently for nine o'clock, then telephoned a colleague at Scotland Yard who owed him a favor, and explained what he wanted. While he waited for a return call he drank three cups of stewed tea, smoked his way through half a packet of cigarettes, and was so unpleasant to his staff that even Maggie Stein kept her tongue in check.

The telephone rang at last, and the man who owed him a favor said, "Well, you may have hit on it. I went through the birth certificates. Plenty of Ryans—Vatican roulette, what? —but none to your purpose. Nor Woods, for that matter. But, as you said, she might have shortened her name, if she's an actress, to make it fit on the marquee. Anyhow, there it was. A girl child called Verity Eleanor Woodhouse was born on April 10, 1951 to one Eleanor Woodhouse, father unknown. Help you at all?"

Inspector Winterkill, subduing any sense of excitement, said with proper Yorkshire caution that it might be just the thing, he would have to check further. Thanks very much, any time he could return the favor . . .

He sat staring at the two names he had written on a sheet of paper, then got up, told Maggie he was going into Rigby and added that, if he turned out to be right, he'd murder the bloody woman himself.

"What woman?"

"Never you mind."

"All right, I won't."

"It's the Jagat case," he said, for he wanted no long-term feud with Maggie Stein. "I think I've got it worked out."

"Have you, then. Well, don't forget you've got a suspect sitting in a cell making all our lives a misery."

"Oh Christ," he muttered, having forgotten all about Bertie de Grey. "Oh, sod him."

After a nasty, chilly week, the weather had turned suddenly into an Indian summer so brilliant and warm that people brought out summer cottons already packed away, and lazy gardeners, who had not yet got around to taking down their gardens, could congratulate themselves on new buddings of roses and ripening of late vegetables, while those like Henry Barnes, who could not abide the straggly look of spent perennials and frost-touched scarlet runners, had to content themselves with pruning their roses and giving the grass a final trim. Still, he was thankful to be able to be out among his flowers. Though with young Selkirk gone there was no longer any need to lock Verity in her room, the strained atmosphere of the house and Verity's woebegone expression made him glad of any excuse to get outside.

Sir Tancred, who usually did not get out of bed until opening time at the White Hart, was awakened by the brilliant sun, and, finding himself unable to get back to sleep, decided to take Baby for a good run on the dales. Blinking a little in the brightness, to which his eyes, attuned to the smoky dusk of the pub, were unaccustomed, he climbed up amid the heather, starting a brace of pheasants who rose with a clatter of wings into the blue air. Baby gave a delighted yelp and charged after them, racial memory leading her to expect the crack of a rifle and a bird tumbling from the sky at any moment. In her enthusiasm she ran all the way to the disused end of the rubbish tip, a place so full of wonderful smells and mysterious sounds that even Sir Tancred's whistle, reminding her that it was nearly eleven and high time they put in an appearance at the White Hart, could not call her back.

"Blast that dog," said her fond owner, and set out down the hill to retrieve her, for Baby was old and rheumatic, and he did not want her to get into an argument with a large and hungry rat.

She was scuffling aside some leaves and whimpering with excitement as he came near. "What have you found then, old girl?" he asked. "Come away now, it's very nearly opening time. What *have* you got there?" Sir Tancred moved closer to look. "Oh my God," he said. "Oh Christ almighty."

The rats had not left enough of the face for it to be recognizable, but the Frye boots, though scarred by sharp teeth, had stood up to attack, and Sir Tancred had seen the jeans and ruffled shirts often enough about town to recognize their tatters and to know to whom they belonged.

It was matinee day, and everyone at the theater was getting ready for the afternoon's performance when Inspector Winterkill arrived. John Silk found his visit mildly inconvenient, but welcomed the inspector with his usual politeness.

"Sorry to bother you, I forgot it was a matinee today," said Inspector Winterkill. "The thing is, I think I've finally worked it all out. Something you said when you were talking about Mrs. Drabble's been bothering me ever since. It's nagged and nagged at me, though I couldn't put my finger on it. Then, suddenly it hit me, right in the middle of—well, never mind that. Ryan—that was a name I should have remembered. He was the chap Mrs. Drabble said came to call on the Barneses just before they acquired a baby."

"Yes, I remember. It's odd, because I had the same feeling of something ringing a bell, but I couldn't track it down, and then I'm afraid I forgot all about it. Yes, Gavin, what is it?"

Gavin, standing in the open door, said there was a problem with one of the spots, and that the new lighting man wouldn't let Barnes near them because he belonged to the carpenters' union and wasn't an electrician.

"Take a pistol from the prop room and threaten to kill him," said John Silk calmly. "It quite often works, the first time, anyhow. Sorry, Winterkill, do please go on about Ryan. Who is he?"

"Someone I should have remembered. He was the alderman who had to resign because he got a little Pierrot dancer with child. Nowadays nobody'd turn a hair, I don't suppose, but back then it was quite a scandal. I don't know how I could have forgotten. Old age, I suppose."

"You mean the baby is Verity Barnes?"

"It happened nineteen years ago. The age just fits."

"Yes, but even if you're right, and I agree it looks very much like it, what can it possibly have to do with Ally?"

"Nothing," said the inspector, looking, thought John, exactly like a not-very-competent magician who had finally managed to pull a rabbit out of his top hat. "Not a bleeding thing. The rat poison was never meant for Mr. Jagat. That's why we couldn't find a motive, of course. The wrong party got the poisoned drink."

"Poor Ally," said John Silk. "What horrid luck. But how fascinating. Are you allowed to tell me whom the poison was meant for? Oh dear. Gavin." His Hamlet appeared once more in the doorway, this time holding a handkerchief to a freely bleeding nose.

"He says that trick's been tried on him before," said Gavin indistinctly through the handkerchief. "He says he doesn't like actors."

"Poor Gavin. I'll go and talk to him."

"No need," said Gavin. "Nigel sorted him out. He boxed at Oxford."

As soon as Gavin had left to put a cold compress on his nose, John Silk turned back to the inspector. "I'm so sorry," he said. "Please forgive all these interruptions. You were saying the arsenic was never intended for Ally."

"That's right. It was the gin made me realize it finally."

"The gin?" said John, a little blankly.

"Yes. The gin in Miss Wood's drink. You remember, someone put gin in her goblet. Everyone thought it was a bad joke, but it occurred to me that perhaps there was more to it than that."

"But why Nell? Oh, I see. You think she was the Pierrot dancer who got pregnant, and therefore the mother of Verity Barnes. How very interesting."

Inspector Winterkill told John of his telephone call to the man in London who owed him a favor, and the result of this man's researches.

"It does sound plausible, doesn't it," said John. "Wait a moment, there's something I want to check." He tilted his chair backward and took down a volume from the shelf behind him. "*Who's Who In The Theater,*" he said. "It's full of the most useful information. Here we are. Woad, Albert—I remember him, just. A very funny Shallow. Wobble, Elvira. I think if I'd been called Wobble I would have taken a stage name." Inspector Winterkill began to fidget. "Wolsey . . . Wood, Eleanor. 'Daughter of Albert Woodhouse and his wife Verity Eleanor.' Verity Eleanor. Well, there you are, Inspector. I shouldn't think that leaves much doubt." John looked up past the inspector to the door Gavin had carelessly left ajar. "Oh dear," he said. "Do come in, Verity."

She entered, looking embarrassed. "I'm ever so sorry," she said, stumbling a little over the words. "I didn't mean—honestly . . ."

"Of course you didn't," said John in his most soothing voice.

The inspector pulled up a chair for her. "Sit down, lass," he said. "Now, how long have you been standing in the doorway?"

"I really didn't mean to listen. I came to tell Mr. Silk that there's been a problem with the lights, but Dad's seeing to it. Only we may have to start a bit late. But I couldn't help overhearing what you said, Mr. Silk. I know it's wrong to listen at doors, but I couldn't make myself go away once I'd started." Tears filled her eyes. "Honestly, Mr. Silk, I'm so sorry."

"I think it was very natural," said John. "I'm only sorry you had to find out like this."

"Oh, that's all right," said Verity, sounding quite happy. "I don't mind. Is it really true, Miss Wood's my mother and Alderman Ryan my father?"

"We're quite sure," the inspector said.

"And I'm not related to the Barneses at all?"

"Not as far as I know."

Verity dropped her face in her hands and let out a great sigh of relief. "Oh, thank God," she said. "Thank God."

John and the inspector looked at each other. John was surprised, and relieved that she was taking it so well, but Inspector Winterkill looked stern. "Now Verity, that's not the way to talk," he admonished. "Mary and Henry Barnes've looked after you since you were a small baby. They've been very good to you. I know you haven't seen eye to eye lately, and I can understand how someone like Miss Wood, an actress, might seem glamorous compared to your mother—to Mary Barnes. But the Barneses have been good parents to you. There's many a girl would be thankful to have parents like that."

Verity had dropped her hands and was looking at the inspector calmly and attentively, like a schoolgirl having a mathematical problem explained to her. Then she nodded. "I know," she said. "Really, I do know. And I am grateful." She got up and turned to John. "I'm sorry I interrupted you. I'll go and see about the lights."

After she had left, John and the inspector sat for a long moment in silence. "Damned if I know what goes on inside their heads," the inspector said finally. "Girls! Do you understand them?"

"I don't suppose they even understand themselves. Look at Nell, staying on here through all this. First someone puts gin in her goblet, presumably hoping she'd go on a toot and get fired. Then all those accidents, sitting down on a broken chair, catching her heel in a torn piece of drugget and falling down stairs. And she must have known the rat poison in Ally's cup was meant for her. Yet she stays on, never saying a word to anyone."

"She could have saved us a lot of trouble if she'd been a bit more talkative," said the inspector crossly. "Maybe she just wanted to be near her daughter."

"Well, she had a powerful incentive not to talk to anyone. Nell the Pierrot girl on Scarborough pier isn't quite how she wanted the world to see her. Tell me, how did Ally get the wrong goblet? He'd made such a fuss about getting the one with the martini in it."

The inspector turned to look at the door, which Verity had closed behind her. "Verity did it," he said. "Oh, quite by accident," he added, seeing John about to protest the very idea of Verity Barnes as a murderess. "I checked the testimony people gave that night. The lights went off and someone jostled the table the drinks were on. Just to make sure, Verity sniffed all the goblets. They were painted black inside, so she couldn't tell by looking. One of them smelled 'nasty'—her word—so she gave that one to Jagat. She didn't know what she'd done until the other night when young Selkirk took her to the Budgie Cage. Beryl and I saw her there. Verity ordered a drink, a martini of all things, never ask me why. I don't suppose she'd ever had anything stronger than a shandy in her entire life before. Anyhow, she picked it up and suddenly got very upset, starting to cry and saying, 'it can't be' or something like that over and over. Beryl thought she was just feeling faint—it's awfully close in there—but it came to me afterwards that that was the first time she'd ever smelled a real gin and French, and suddenly she realized that it was nothing like the drink she'd given Jagat."

"Poor Ally. When was that, by the way, the visit to the Budgie Cage?"

"Oh, Saturday week, I think. Yes. Saturday."

"That would fit. She's been strange all this week, very

mopy, doesn't hear what you say to her, goes about like Ophelia looking for a convenient river. I put it down to Selkirk's abrupt departure. But of course it might have been the discovery that, however inadvertently, she caused Ally's death."

"Or both," said the inspector. "A broken heart and a death on her conscience. Poor lass. So there you have it, you see. Nell Wood turns up, quarrels with Mary Barnes—not about mending a wooden box, as she claimed, but about making herself known as Verity's mother. Someone puts gin or rat poison in her drink. Nothing happens, so someone tries again. Ally Jagat gets the drink by mistake, and it kills him. We have the motive, the opportunity, and the means. They all point to one person. Mary Barnes protecting her young."

John Silk sighed. "I wish I could disagree with you. I shall never get a cleaning woman as thorough as Mrs. Barnes again." The telephone on his desk began to ring. He picked it up. "Yes," he said, "the inspector is right here." He handed over the telephone. "Gaskell."

"Yes, what is it?" asked the inspector, who always found it difficult to be civil to the officious young constable. "What? Yes, I'll be right over. And try and keep it quiet, for heaven's sake. We don't want to have all Rigby turning out to gawk." He returned the telephone to John Silk. "They've found Selkirk," he said. "He's dead."

The inspector might as well have saved his breath, warning Gaskell not to talk, not because the constable was an incurable gossip—indeed, he'd only had time to tell the exciting news to his mother and his girlfriend before calling the inspector—but because in small towns like Rigby gossip does not travel from house to house and street to street, but falls in a mysterious pentecostal way on every part of town at once. By the time the police ambulance drove slowly up the High Street, doorsteps which had already been swept once that morning, were receiving a second going-over at the hands of careful housewives; tablecloths, shaken free of crumbs directly after breakfast, were waved from windows once again; brass doorplates, already shiny with polish, were rubbed anew. Even the habitues of the White Hart and the Theater Pub, who never saw daylight during legal drinking hours, took their pints to the sidewalk, ostensibly to enjoy the rays of the sun. Only Mr. Barnes, absorbed in untangling a number of spaghetti-like wires, and Gavin, trying with every trick of make-up to reduce his swollen tomato nose to something more suitable to a *jeune premier,* took no part in the general excitement.

"They do say," said Mrs. Shrubsole with relish, "that there wasn't nothing left of his face, not to speak of, anyroad."

" 'Is fingers was all gnawed away," someone in the crowd contributed.

"I 'eard they could only identify 'im by 'is boots," said another, adding to the general enjoyment.

"Why, what's happened? What's the matter?" Verity asked. She was on her way to the Theater Pub to fetch a Scotch egg and half a pint of ale for Gavin Beauclerc, who did not want to appear in public until his nose had subsided.

"It's 'im, young Selkirk," said Mrs. Shrubsole, rushing to get in ahead of everyone else with her ghoulish news. "They've found 'im at the tip. Dreadful, it was. They do say the rats 'ad been at 'im for days."

Mildred, the barmaid at the Theater Pub, put an arm round Verity's shoulders, thinking the girl might faint. "It wouldn't hurt you to watch your tongue, Lola Shrubsole," she said sharply, "at least once every ten years or so." In a much kinder voice she said to Verity, "Come inside, luv, and have a drink. You look as if you could do with a drop."

The ambulance had moved out of sight, and the regulars, seeing no further reason to stand outside, returned to the pub, where Mildred ignored their calls for refills while she pushed Verity into a chair and brought her a glass of brandy.

"Is it true?" Verity asked. "What Auntie Lola said."

"I'm afraid so, luv. Have a drop of brandy, it'll do you good."

"But what happened? Why was he at the tip? I don't understand."

"I'm not sure," said Mildred. "They say he was hit on the head. So at least he was dead before—well, never mind. Just tip that brandy back, you'll feel better."

Verity drank obediently, coughed, sputtered and was given a glass of water. "That's better," said Mildred, pleased with the result, and went to wait on her other customers. Verity continued to sit in the corner where Mildred had pushed her into a chair. She did not cry but simply sat, looking at the table in front of her, where a reflection of the brandy made a dancing spot of light on the wooden surface. There was a small frown between her brows; a frown her teachers would have recognized as Verity Barnes making her careful way through a problem in arithmetic or an assignment on how she had spent her summer vacation. Just before Mildred got ready to call "Time, gentlemen," she got up.

"Alright, luv?"

"Yes. Thanks, Mildred. I haven't got my purse, but I'll pay you later."

"Don't be daft. Go on home and have a bit of lie-down, why don't you? They can get on at the theater without you for once."

"Thanks ever so," Verity said politely. Mildred watched her turn into the High Street, and assumed she had gone home, until Mrs. Barnes came pounding on the back door after closing time, saying Verity was nowhere to be found; she had not gone back to the theater, nor was she at home, and had Mildred any idea where she could be.

CHAPTER XII

Verity Barnes walked into the Scarborough police station. She was neatly dressed in the pale blue suit she wore to church on Sunday, and carried a small overnight case. Maggie Stein was at the desk. She looked at the young girl, wondering what she could possibly want in a police station. Verity put the overnight case on the floor and said, "Could I see Inspector Winterkill, please. My name is Verity Barnes."

"The inspector isn't in right now. Can I help you?" said Maggie.

"I don't know." Verity's voice was calm; there was no trace of hysteria in it. "Perhaps you can. I want to give myself up. You see, I killed Tim Selkirk and Mr. Jagat."

They were very nice to her. Maggie even went so far as to make a fresh pot of tea, something she never did if there was a man about. Verity accepted a cup gratefully. Her mouth was so dry she thought she would not have been able to speak without it.

They did not in any case let her speak until they had tracked down Inspector Winterkill. Maggie suggested she should have her parents present, but at this Verity showed, for the first time since she had entered the police station, such signs of distress and indeed hysteria that Maggie said, "Never mind, then, luv, we won't do anything you don't want."

Inspector Winterkill was not so obliging. The first thing he did was to telephone the Rigby police and tell Constable Gaskell to find the Barneses and bring them to Scarborough.

"I've come to give myself up," Verity said to the inspector. She had known him all her life and felt comfortable with him. "I killed Mr. Jagat and Tim Selkirk, you see." She took a sip of tea. "Only please don't tell Mum and Dad. They'd want to come and see me, and I couldn't bear it, really I couldn't."

"Reet, lass," said the inspector, who rarely lapsed into the speech of his childhood except as a joke or in bed with Beryl. "Just take your time and tell us what happened."

"I didn't mean to do it," Verity said, and Maggie, suspecting there was a man behind her trouble, as there was behind most trouble in the world, said, "Of course not, luv," and was scowled at by the inspector.

"It was the drink, you see," said Verity. "Mr. Jagat's, I mean. He was always so nice, and it worried me that he was drinking too much. I knew Mum had some stuff—it's called Antabuse, from America—she used to give Dad." She blushed deeply at having brought out this skeleton from the family closet. "Dad used to take a drop too much," she said, "but it was a long time ago, before I was born. Only Mum kept it by her, just in case. Sometimes when Dad went out with the British Legion she'd say, 'Now, remember, Dad,' and hold up the bottle and we'd all laugh ever so, because of course he didn't any more—drink, I mean."

"So you thought if you put some in Mr. Jagat's gin, he'd stop drinking too."

Verity nodded. The young constable who was taking down her confession in shorthand, thought her the prettiest girl he'd ever seen. To show his admiration he pushed a plate of stale buns in her direction. Verity did not appear to notice.

"When you found it was rat poison in Mr. Jagat's drink," the inspector asked severely, "why didn't you come and tell me?"

"I couldn't see what good it would do," Verity said reasonably. "It wasn't as if I'd meant to kill him and needed to be punished, was it?" This had a rehearsed sound, and Inspector Winterkill wondered whether it had come from Mrs. Barnes.

The whole story sounded unlikely, though he supposed it was possible. He had never come across Antabuse before, but it would be easy enough to find out what it looked like. Rat poison was invariably dyed, so that it could not accidentally be confused with any other white, grainy substance, such as sugar. Inspector Winterkill very much doubted that Antabuse would prove to be a blue powder that would have allowed the mix-up Verity laid claim to.

"How do you think the rat poison got into the Antabuse bottle?" he asked.

Verity shrugged. "I don't know. People do put things into jars and bottles where they don't belong, don't they?"

Indeed they did, thought the inspector. Warn the silly buggers as much as you liked, they still moved pills and medicines from their rightful containers, put bits of leftover cleaning fluid into milk bottles and weed killer into jam jars, and poisoned themselves nine times out of ten because they couldn't bear to leave things in the clearly labelled containers in which they had been bought.

"What about Selkirk?" Inspector Winterkill asked. She'd had time to rehearse her story of Ally Jagat's death—he suspected that she had done so ever since the day she had discovered that she was not the Barnes's real daughter—and she had not come up with anything very convincing. He wondered what she would do with the far more shocking death of a boy she had fancied, of which she had first heard only an hour or so ago.

"Oh, it's him I've really come about," said Verity, her voice eager. "I didn't mean to kill Mr. Jagat, and actually he died of a heart attack, so it wasn't my fault, was it, and I couldn't see what good it would be, me spending my life in jail over what was really an accident. But I killed Tim. And so of course I ought to be punished for that."

"I see." Inspector Winterkill was always at his best at times like these. When everyone else wanted to scream or shake the person being questioned for his want of logic or knowledge of the law, he simply plodded on, bovine and patient, letting the suspect talk rubbish for hours if necessary, until he got what he wanted. "Tell us what happened then, lass," he said, using his comfortable Rigby voice.

"Dad said I wasn't to see him any more," said Verity. "Dad said Tim wasn't to be trusted. When I told him—told Tim, I mean—he said to meet him just once more. To say goodbye, like." She drank her tepid tea. Her voice had gone dry and hoarse.

"Go on, luv," Inspector Winterkill said.

"We always met by the old plane spotting shelter on top of Rigby Dale," Verity said. "I told Tim I'd come there, but it was to be for the last time, just to say goodbye, nothing else. He agreed and we met there last Tuesday after tea."

"Did your parents know?"

"Oh no. Dad would never have let me go. He'd have locked me in my room."

Verity cleared her throat and Maggie poured her the last, stewed dregs of tea. "Go on, luv, get it off your chest," she encouraged. "You'll feel all the better for it." As she had suspected all along, a man was at the bottom of the trouble.

"Well, we met," said Verity. "That's all, really. I killed him."

"Come, you don't just meet people and murder them," said the inspector patiently. "You're not a psychopath, Verity. You must have had a reason."

Verity blushed the exact shade of the pink angora pullover she wore. "He—he tried to take advantage of me."

The inspector thought how quaint and positively Victorian that phrase was. Surely no one had used it for years.

"There," said Maggie, her theories borne out, "just as I thought."

The young constable, overcome by admiration of Verity's modest ways, had lost track of his notes and hastened to catch up.

"Can you describe what happened, Verity," the inspector asked. "Just how did you kill him?"

Verity looked disconcerted, like a child in school who is called upon to answer a question on a subject she'd forgotten to prepare. "I know it's difficult to have to go over anything so upsetting, Verity," Inspector Winterkill said kindly. "I wouldn't ask you to, but you have to understand that we have to have all the information in a case like this."

Verity nodded. "It's like what I said. He was trying to take advantage of me."

"Just how did he do that?"

Verity looked pleadingly at Maggie Stein, who said, "Don't be embarrassed, luv. Just go ahead and tell us. We've heard it all before."

"Well, it's just . . . you know . . . he pushed me down and . . ." she looked from the inspector to Maggie, blushing ever more deeply, "I think I screamed, but of course up there no one would hear. Then I suddenly felt a stone under my hand and I picked it up and hit him on the head. Of course," she added earnestly, "I didn't mean to kill him. I just wanted him to let me go."

"Of course," said the inspector. "I'm sure no one can blame you for that. Can you tell me just where you hit him? What part of the head?"

Verity closed her eyes. Two tears found their way between her lashes. "I can't . . ."

"Just take your time."

She shook her head, more tears following the first two. Maggie put an arm around her and stroked her soft hair. "Take your time, luv, we've all afternoon," said the inspector. It sounded like comfort, but was clearly meant to tell her he was not about to stop until he had all the information he wanted. The young constable said "Have a toffee," and held it out on the flat of his hand, as if he were feeding sugar to a horse.

"That's enough, Frank," said the inspector. "Now, Verity, would you like to stop for a few minutes?"

Verity shook her head and blew her nose into a tissue Maggie had handed her. "I'd like to tell you now. To be done with it."

"That's right. Now you say you hit Selkirk on the head with a stone. Just where did you hit him?"

Verity shut her eyes as if trying to remember. "Here," she said, touching the back of her head.

"And then you dragged him to the tip?"

"Oh no. No, not till after dark. I just covered him over with some twigs and heather."

"Weren't you at all afraid of the rats?"

"Well, I'm used to them, you see."

"Yes, I suppose you are. Wasn't it difficult, dragging a dead body?"

"It was downhill all the way."

"Yes, of course. And so you covered him over with rubbish and went home and to bed. Did you say anything to your mother?"

She shook her head.

"Not then or at any time?"

"Never."

"Now, Verity," said Inspector Winterkill, "you know that it's a crime to lie to the police. Is everything you have told us the truth and nothing but the truth?"

She looked at him, a panicky, trapped look, but she said calmly, "Yes, it is."

"All right. Your confession will be typed up, then you can read it over carefully, and if everything is as you said it, you can sign it. Constable Stein will take you to a cell. I don't want to upset you, Verity, but we've sent for your parents. If you don't want to see them you don't have to, but they're on their way here. Now, don't take on so, lass, there now, you must have known we couldn't just leave it without calling your parents." If only they wouldn't cry, the inspector thought, annoyed. "Maggie'll see that you're all right. Have another cup of tea and quiet down a bit, there's a good girl." He patted her vaguely on the head and left the room, shutting the door with a sigh of relief. In a few minutes Maggie came into his office and let the door slam behind her.

"Why did you do that?"

"Do what?"

"Put that poor little idiot through a false confession. You know there wasn't a word of truth in anything she said. Selkirk wasn't hit on the back of the head, but on top, and he wasn't hit with a stone, if the fracture is anything to go by. And can you picture that child dragging him over hill and dale and leaving him for a rats' dinner? Even *you* can't possibly believe any of that."

Inspector Winterkill resented that "even you." He would have liked to remind Maggie Stein that such behavior to an inspector from a mere constable was highly improper, but could not think of a way of phrasing it that would not bring a balls-crushing retort.

"I know she didn't do it," he said. "And I think I know who did. But I haven't any proof. I'm hoping that my keeping Verity locked up and pretending to believe her story will make the guilty party give herself away."

For the first time Maggie Stein looked at him with interest. "You mean Mary Barnes."

He nodded.

"But why?"

"Someone dragged dirt on her rug."

"What?"

"It's something my former wife said. She said she thought anyone could kill, given the right circs. I'd just come from the Barneses, and she said yes, she thought Mary Barnes might kill if someone tracked dirt on her rug. Someone did." He told Maggie what he had discovered, omitting John Silk's trip to Brighton, having indeed forgotten for the moment that small but vital contribution.

"But why would that poor child confess to those two murders?"

"I think she's paying off her debts. When she accidentally discovered that she wasn't the Barnes's daughter, she said, 'Thank God.' I think she suspected from the start that her mother was involved in it somehow, and I suppose she thought it was better to be the daughter of a Pierrot dancer and a lecherous alderman than to have a murderess for a mother. At the time it didn't strike me. Indeed, I reminded her that she owed the Barneses a lot, and she agreed. So she's discharging her debts."

"The poor little idiot," said Maggie, just as the young constable opened the door and said, "Mrs. Barnes is here, sir."

Mary Barnes brushed him aside as if he were a pesky fly and walked up to the desk.

"Well, Harold, what's all this nonsense about Verity?"

The inspector stood up. "She's confessed to the murders of Mr. Jagat and Tim Selkirk, Mary."

"And you believed her! Really, Harold. I've known you since you were so high, and a very silly child you were. It doesn't look as if you've improved much."

"We have the confession, Mary," said the inspector stolidly. "Why do you suppose she told us all those stories if they weren't true?"

"Let me go to her. I'll soon sort her out."

"She may not want to see you, Mary. She's said she doesn't want to see anyone. But there's nothing against your trying. Constable Stein'll show you the way."

Maggie got to her feet and Mrs. Barnes followed her down the hallway, past a cell housing a drunk sleeping off the previous evening's celebrations, and two young men with shaggy Beatle haircuts and badly bruised faces stemming from an altercation over the ownership of a certain young lady who couldn't make up her mind. Mrs. Barnes averted her eyes from them and pinched her nostrils as if she were smelling something so unspeakable that a decent woman had no recourse except to pretend that the noisome object did not exist at all. Maggie wondered whether she had any idea that she would soon be occupying a cell herself. As they turned the corner she said, "Please, Mrs. Barnes, wait here for a moment. I'll tell Verity you want to see her."

Mrs. Barnes was about to protest, but the calm assurance of Constable Stein reminded her that she was not on her home ground, and she remained silent.

Verity was sitting on the cot in her cell as if she had not moved since they had left her there. She looked composed and calm, and even managed to smile when she saw Maggie, but the moment her mother's name was mentioned she burst into tears and shrank into the corner of the cot as if she hoped she could make herself small enough to become invisible.

"There, luv," Maggie said kindly. Generally she had very little use for silly, fluffy bits of girls like Verity Barnes, and thought they deserved what they usually got—marriage and the privilege of waiting on a man hand and foot for the rest of their lives—but there was something about Verity that called out her chivalrous instincts. "You don't have to see anyone you don't want to." She took a neatly folded handkerchief from the sleeve of her uniform—a piece of military swank that always annoyed the very devil out of the inspector—and gave it to Verity. "Don't go on so, luv, you'll give yourself a frightful headache," she said. "Here, blow your nose and I'll tell your mum you can't see her just now."

"There is no need to tell me anything," said Mrs. Barnes, standing in the open door of the cell. "Now, Verity, what is all this nonsense?"

Verity stopped crying so suddenly that it seemed to Maggie as if someone had turned off a tap and stopped her tears. In a voice that squeaked and shook, she said, "I don't want to see you ever again."

"It's your mother, Verity," said Maggie. "Don't talk to her like that."

"She isn't my mother. Miss Wood is. I heard Inspector Winterkill tell Mr. Silk at the theater."

"So you know," said Mrs. Barnes. She was very pale, but her voice was calm. "It's quite true. Barnes and I adopted you when you were a baby. There's nothing wrong with that. Certainly it's no excuse to refuse to speak to me, or to go confessing to two murders you never committed."

"Don't you see?" said Verity, beginning to sob again. "That's why. You don't understand. I did it because I wasn't your daughter. You've been so good to me all these years. I didn't know how else to pay you back."

They were so intent on one another that they had forgotten Maggie's presence. Knowing what she knew, she studied Mrs. Barnes with both sympathy and interest. In her short time with the police Maggie had encountered violence and murderous rage, but never a respectable woman who had coolly put rat poison in the drink of a well-known actor, and hit a young man over the head with the proverbial blunt instrument, and dragged him to the rubbish tip to leave him to the rats. Mrs. Barnes wore her summer churchgoing clothes; a dress of blue-and-white spotted silk, and a blue straw hat of depressing design. Her gloves, bag and shoes were immaculately white. Never had Maggie seen anyone look so intimidatingly respectable.

"Well, thank you *very* much," said Mrs. Barnes. "A fine thanks I call it, telling lies to the police and dragging our good name in the mud. Whatever made you do it?"

Verity wept with the vexation that comes to those who find their grand gesture of self-sacrifice not very much appreciated by the recipient. "That's not fair," she said, showing temper for the first time. "It's not. You kill two people and then you accuse me of dragging our name in the mud. It's not fair, Mum."

Except for her pallor, Mrs. Barnes had until that moment seemed admirably calm. She belonged to a generation and class that had been taught to keep its feelings hidden, Maggie knew, her own parents being much the same. "Never give yourself away to strangers," would have been the motto on their coat of arms, if they had owned one.

But at Verity's accusation the starch went out of Mary Barnes. She groped behind her, felt the hard, narrow prison cot and collapsed on it. When she finally spoke she sounded as if someone had hit her in the stomach, knocking the wind out of her.

"I! You think I killed them?"

Verity was past speech. She nodded. A little wail caught in her throat. "You didn't? You truly didn't?" Weeping and incoherent, she hugged Mrs. Barnes. "Oh Mum, I'm sorry, I'm sorry."

Mrs. Barnes blinked back tears. Awkwardly stroking Verity's hair, she said, "I've told you a hundred times if I've told you once, Verity, don't call me Mum. It's low."

"You didn't, truly? I thought you—you were the last one off the stage that night, don't you remember? You were nearly caught when the curtain went up. I didn't think anything of it then, not even when they found out poor Mr. Jagat died of rat poison. It wasn't till I found a bit of a poison-pen letter in the rubbish, and then at the memorial service, when Mr. Silk imitated him, remember, you turned so white, it was like the play in *Hamlet,* when King Claudius can't bear it a moment longer and shouts for light . . ."

Mrs. Barnes shook her head. She had never troubled herself to watch any of the plays. She was at the theater to clean. What went on on stage was no business of hers.

"I couldn't imagine why you'd want to kill Mr. Jagat, but I thought you had. When it came out he'd died of a heart attack, really, not poison, I was so relieved for a bit. That's why I went out with Tim first, I thought he must be so lonely, you'd taken away his . . ." she could not bring herself to use the word "lover" to her mother ". . . his friend. And then when I realized that I'd mixed up the goblets, that the poison hadn't been meant for Mr. Jagat at all, and right after that I overheard the inspector telling Mr. Silk about Miss Wood being my mother, well, it all started to make sense." The quiet child, so shy as a rule, could not stop herself talking. All the dreadful secrets she had carried with her these weeks dropped like stones from her heart, leaving it lighter and lighter. Both Maggie and Mrs. Barnes had the good sense to let her be, sensing how much this spate of words eased her. "Then, when Tim's body was found today I was sure it had to be you. And this time I couldn't say it was an accident. It was all my fault. You and Dad told me to stop seeing him, and I wouldn't. If I'd obeyed you he'd never have been killed. And I thought, no matter what you'd done, how good you've been to me when I wasn't even your own, and how in a way it really was my fault, so I came and gave myself up. Oh, I've been so wicked, Mum. Can you forgive me?"

Mrs. Barnes released herself from her daughter's damp embrace, but there was nothing unloving in the way she pushed her away. The handkerchief Maggie had given Verity had been wept and sniffled into well past its usefulness. Mrs. Barnes opened her purse and took out a square of the whitest linen. As if Verity were a little child, she wiped her eyes, and blew her nose. She found a comb in her bag and pulled it carefully through Verity's soft, dishevelled hair. This done she neatly put the comb and handkerchief away and snapped shut her purse.

"Now," she said, "that's enough. You've had a good cry, Verity, and as for the rest, what you thought of me, we'll forgive and forget. It was a natural mistake, anyone could have made it. I never killed Mr. Jagat, or Tim Selkirk, you believe that now, don't you?" Verity nodded. Her eyes filled again with tears. "Now, no more of that," said Mrs. Barnes. "You'll have to pull yourself together, Verity, because I've got a shock for you. I didn't kill them, you see, but I know who did."

Both Maggie and Verity looked at her in silence. "I don't

understand," said Verity. "What are you saying? Whom are you talking about, Mum? Who was it?"

"Haven't you guessed yet, you little silly. It was Barnes, of course. Your Dad."

CHAPTER XIII

"Of course I never meant to kill Mr. Jagat," said Barnes. "It was an accident. Selkirk was different. I killed him for good reason, but look at it as you will, it was murder." He sat on a hard, wooden chair in John Silk's office, facing him across his desk. In his lap he held a revolver. John would have given a good deal to know whether it was a real one or came from the prop room. Guns used in plays were outwardly identical with the real thing, the only difference being that they could not commit murder. Barnes, he knew, had been in the war, and though army rules required that all guns be returned to store at the end of national service, a good many people would appear to have managed to keep souvenirs.

"T' missus and I talked it over," said Barnes, sounding very calm and reasonable. I'm going to take the five o'clock bus into Scarborough to give myself up." He pronounced it "oop," the only sign to show that he was under stress, for Mrs. Barnes did not like her family to talk "Yorkshire."

"As I said, Mr. Jagat was an accident. It could have happened to anybody. But Selkirk was murder, so it's only proper I should be tried. He were vexing the missus, being after Verity the way he was, and I won't have that," said Barnes, making it sound as if he had merely given Tim Selkirk a good talking to, instead of smashing his skull and dragging him down to the tip for the rats to tear apart. "I won't have anybody vexing Mother," he said again.

"Oh yes, quite," said John, keeping his voice as calm as Barnes's, doing his best not to allow his eyes to stray to the gun, which was unmistakably pointed at him.

"Of course I could have taken the three o'clock bus," said

Barnes, "but I told Mother I had something to settle with you. There's two people dead, one by accident, one not. And none of it would have happened but for you. You started it, bringing them here, Jagat and that Selkirk, and her who's no better than she should be."

John, though very frightened, tried to disentangle from Barnes's mad logic a thread of reason. "Her?" he asked, though of course he knew.

"That Miss Wood. It's no use pretending with me, Mr. Silk. I know what you went to Brighton to find out."

"I didn't find out much," said John, taking care to say neither too much nor too little. If he pretended to know nothing at all, Barnes might well decide to leave it at that and dry up. If he pretended to know more than he knew, the result would be the same. He remembered reading once that when captives under torture or long interrogation at last give up and confess, they get an almost voluptuous feeling of pleasure from talking. Perhaps Barnes too, having once told his story to his wife, had felt the lust for confession. He gave no appearance of being in a hurry, seemed indeed content to sit and talk till the five o'clock bus was due. Playing for time, John knew, was his one hope. At any moment someone on an errand connected with theater business might put his head round the door, distracting Barnes for the brief moment needed to throw the heavy Georgian inkpot at his head. "All I heard," John said, "was that Mrs. Barnes badly wanted a baby and couldn't have one, so that Verity was likely to be an adopted child. I don't somehow think anyone would commit murder because I'd found out that much, do you?"

"Well, not if that was all," said Barnes. It seemed that John's guess had been a good one, for Barnes added, "You know that much, you might as well know the rest." John wondered whether it would be a good idea to offer him a drink. He had heard the occasional rumor that Barnes had had a problem with alcohol in his younger years. Certainly he had never been seen to have more than a very occasional half pint at the Theater Pub, and that only if someone else was paying and Mrs. Barnes was nowhere in sight. A big Scotch with very little water might fuddle him enough to spoil his aim or cause him to lose sight of his errand altogether.

Since he had never seen Barnes drunk, John unfortunately had no way of telling how drink would take him. Would he become cheerful, sentimental, weepy, or belligerent? Since very mild, repressed people often, in John's experience, turned angry, even violent when their inhibitions were blunted by alcohol, he decided that Barnes would probably be better without. A pity, he thought. He could have done with a large whiskey himself.

As he sat, weighing these possibilities, Barnes, usually such a silent man, had embarked on his story, going back to his undistinguished wartime service with the Green Howards while Mary had worked in a canteen in a big hotel in Brighton taken over by the army. The boarding house had been Mrs. Barnes's idea. Once the war was over, she had reasoned, people would feel the need for a change, for taking that long-postponed holiday. Since foreign travel would be out of the question for some time to come, what better than a vacation by the seaside. Anyone with rooms to let would be bound to make money. With their combined wartime savings they had been able to put a down payment on a run-down bed-and-breakfast that was going cheap.

What with Barnes's carpentry skills and Mary's splendid housekeeping, they soon had it, as Barnes put it, "all shipshape," and were doing very well indeed. When foreign travel once again became possible, the amount of currency people were allowed to take out of the country was so small that many opted for another summer by the sea, and the Wellington was invariably filled to the last room.

This was all terribly dull, John felt, but was grateful for Barnes's loquacity nevertheless. "Keep on talking, old dear," he silently told the little man with the gun in his lap. "Tell me about those beastly postwar boarding house breakfasts, the troubles with the hot water, the rainy days with sandy, cross children kept indoors. Don't stop, old darling, just go on."

All had gone well, Barnes said, except for one thing. Mary had wanted a baby; not just wanted, but pined, yearned, longed for a child until she was fretted away to a shadow.

John had heard this part of the story already from Mrs. Drabble, but so eager was he for Barnes to keep talking that he nodded sympathetically as he was taken on a second guided tour of Mrs. Barnes's plumbing, and the variety and helplessness of the doctors they had visited. Barnes talked like a Trappist who has just fled the monastery, as drunk on the sudden flow of words as he might have been on John Silk's whiskey. A habitually silent man, he had lived for weeks with the secret of murder bottled up inside him. Now that he had begun to talk he would no doubt do so again, to the Scarborough police, except that by then he would have a third murder to add to his confession. John felt a clammy shiver run down his spine. "Yes," he said, his voice muted and sympathetic. "Oh yes, quite."

One day an alderman from Rigby, one Bill Ryan, had come to see the Barneses at their place in Brighton. "You wouldn't know him," said Barnes. "He was before your time. His wife was a cousin to Mary. Still is, I suppose. A nasty shrewish besom, but Mary always said family's family, and kept in touch with her. That's how Glenda knew how much Mary wanted a baby, and Bill knew where to find us."

Not that Ryan had come to the point right away, Barnes said. He had talked about the weather, rationing, the state of the world and other trivial matters. But in the end it all came out. It was about a baby that Alderman Ryan had come to see the Barneses. He had, he confessed, with a great many arrumphs, hems and haws, got a girl in trouble. A girl, plainly, who was no better than she should be, an actress, as a matter of fact, or rather, not even an actress, but a dancer with a Pierrot troupe that entertained trippers on Scarborough pier.

"Nell Wood," said John.

"That's right. Her la-de-da ladyship in person. She didn't want the baby, not her, and that was why Ryan came to see us. He didn't want the child put up for adoption; he wanted a decent Yorkshire family to raise her, people who were chapel and knew what was right and proper. And though he said nowt, I don't reckon he wanted to go to an adoption agency and have his name put down, him being an alderman. Some of the story leaked out later for all he was so careful. You can't stop gossip, can you? The girl's name didn't come out, she'd disappeared by then, and nobody but us knew what happened to the baby, but there was just enough talk for Ryan to have to leave town.

"We talked it over for a long time, me and Mary," said Barnes. "What with the bad blood on her mother's side, I wasn't sure we ought to take a chance, but Mary was pining for a baby of her own till she was nowt but skin and bones, so I said let's give it a try. We never regretted raising Verity. She grew up a good, decent girl; you'd hardly know her mother was that kind of woman. We'd be happy to this day if it hadn't been for you, Mr. Silk, bringing her here to this very theater."

"But I knew nothing about any of this," protested John. "Miss Wood's coming here was the merest coincidence."

"Some might see it that way," said Barnes. "I don't."

Better in that case to keep him talking, John thought. Time was his only hope. Someone was bound to open the office door sooner or later. Pretending ignorance, he said, "But what had Ally Jagat to do with any of it? I simply don't understand."

"Nowt," said Barnes. "I've told you. He were an accident."

"Yes. But how did it happen?"

"The rat poison was never meant for him. It was for her, just like the gin. I tried that first, after she came to me and told me who she was. She claimed she wouldn't tell Verity, she just wanted to have her to tea, become acquainted, like, she said. Stupid, I call it. What would people think, the likes of her and a young girl working in the theater. I told her it wouldn't do. 'It doesn't seem an unreasonable request,' she says to me." The little carpenter did a very good imitation of Nell as Gwendolen Fairfax. In spite of his precarious position, John could not help smiling. "You may laugh," said Barnes, "but it was no laughing matter to me. 'Please don't force me to take legal steps,' she said. 'I want us to be friends.'"

"How did she come to be so sure Verity was her daughter?" asked John. "I can't say I ever noticed any physical resemblance."

"Well, Ryan had promised us he'd never tell her, but he must have after all. Most likely she wormed it out of him."

John found himself getting very annoyed at the unfairness of the little man. Everything was Nell's fault. Nell was no better than she should be, Nell wormed secrets out of Ryan while he, an alderman who had seduced a fifteen-year-old girl and had broken his promise to keep a secret, came up smelling like a rose. Poor Nell. What a long way this sordid story was from Mummy and the family Lowestoft. What a compelling dream that upper middle-class family must have been for the desperate, pregnant little dancer, for her to have carried it off as real for all these years with never a slip. Well, one perhaps. When she had tasted the gin in Gertrude's goblet, she'd said, "Crikey, it's gin," in tones of purest cockney. Poor Nell. Fancy my offering her a job in Rigby. She'd hesitated a long time before accepting it. John had thought at the time that she preferred not to leave London for a drafty little Yorkshire town, but he now pictured to himself the struggle she must have gone through before she had said regally, "It might be rather fun. How very kind of you to think of me, Johnny."

"I begged her not to tell the missus," said Barnes. " 'You don't give me much choice,' she told me and sure enough she came round to the house one day when she knew I was at the theater. Well, Mother sent her off with a flea in her ear. But all the same, she was frightened. When I came home I found her crying to beat the band. Oh, she took on something terrible, blaming herself for letting Verity work at the theater, for never going through with a legal adoption. You see, Mr. Silk, I don't like to have Mother upset."

There was something impressive in such single-mindedness, thought John, even if at the moment it was pointing a gun at his heart. A life built around the sole object of keeping vexation from Mrs. Barnes might seem limited to a more ordinary person, but it could also be taken as the sign of a deep and abiding love. Films and television, thought John, have taught us to think of lovers in a certain way; as young, handsome, glamorous, and usually possessed of the outward signs of wealth. The mousy little carpenter and his dried-up stick of a wife were no Paolo and Francesca, no Romeo and Juliet. Yet Barnes forewent one of his few pleasures—a pint with his mates in the pub—in a life which could not contain many, and had plotted and carried out two murders (even if one was accidental) to preserve Mary Barnes's peace of mind. How endlessly interesting marriages were, thought John, a lifelong bachelor, and how closed to the outside view, except when something drastic and unexpected like murder drew aside the curtain and gave you a momentary glimpse inside.

"So I took steps," said Barnes. First had come the gin. If Nell inadvertently drank it and went on a toot, as he put it, she might lose her job and leave town. Unfortunately for all concerned this mild stratagem had failed. So Barnes had progressed to the more serious weapon of rat poison. "Not enough to kill her, mind," he earnestly assured John, just enough to have her doubled over with the world's worst bellyache for a few days. After she'd recovered, Barnes had planned to send her an anonymous letter, warning her that this was just the beginning, that next time she would not get off so easily. "It's simple," said Barnes, and described the method he had watched on the telly. "You cut words from the newspapers and glue them on the writing paper. But when Mr. Jagat drank the poison by mistake, I thought it was getting too risky to send the letter, so I tore it up and tried to burn it in the ashtray. But just then Mother called me and said what was I doing, having a fag when I know she doesn't like me smoking in the house and anyway tea was ready. So I put it in the rubbish and left it for later. When I got back to it a piece was missing. I've wondered many and many a time who found it."

"I see," said John, wondering whether anyone was ever again going to come to his office door. Usually he found it difficult to put in even an hour or two of work, and often he silently cursed the constant interruptions, but now, when he longed for anyone, even Mrs. Shrubsole, to knock on the door, ready to recite one of her endless and boring complaints, he might as well have been in quarantine with bubonic plague, for all the visitors he got.

Barnes was coming to the end of his story and he, John, had still no more practical plan of escape than to hope that something, anything, would distract Barnes long enough for him to throw the inkwell at the man.

"Well, when Mr. Jagat died, Mother and me talked it over," Barnes said. "I thought I should give myself up, even though it was an accident, but Mother said there was no need to disgrace the family over something I hadn't intended and couldn't help."

The reasoning behind this seemed peculiar to John, but he was not about to argue with someone pointing a gun at him. "I wasn't easy in my mind about it," said Barnes, "but when the verdict was brought in that Mr. Jagat had died of a heart attack, I had to agree with Mother. All the same I was sorry. Mr. Jagat was always a very kind and pleasant gentleman."

"Indeed he was," John agreed.

"Well, then our Verity started to keep company with that Tim Selkirk. We didn't like it, Mother and me, but seeing that he'd come here with Mr. Jagat, we thought she wouldn't come to any harm. Mother said better him than someone like Mr. Pratt, if you take my meaning.

"But then we read the stories in the papers about him and those models, if that's what you want to call them. You can't believe everything you read in the papers, but if half of those stories were true, I said to Mother, he was not the right young man for our Verity. She's got to stop seeing him, I said. So Mother told her, at the theater it was, between the matinee and the evening performance. And that night, when I came home, I found Mother sitting in our bedroom, still with her overall on, just staring at the wall. 'She knows', she said to me. 'Verity knows.' 'Knows what?' I said, but I knew what she meant all right. 'Verity knows you put the poison in Mr. Jagat's drink. I tried to talk to her about seeing that young Selkirk, and she said to me, "You know why I'm going to keep on seeing Tim, and you know why you can't stop me." She's got a piece of that letter too, the one with the words cut from the papers. It'd fallen behind the bench and she found it when she was cleaning up. She knows.'

" 'Well then, I'll go and give myself up,' I said. 'That'll put an end to the business.' 'And have it all come out, about that woman and everything,' she said. 'Don't be daft.' We were up half the night, talking it over. Finally we decided to let things be for the moment. 'Verity's a good girl,' Mother said. 'She won't come to any harm. If it comes out about Miss Wood, and you killing Mr. Jagat by mistake, she'll never get a decent chap. That Selkirk's a fly-by-night, he won't be here long.' I agreed with her, not to upset her more, but I couldn't help remembering the bad blood Verity had from her mother. Still, it seemed all right at first. I kept an eye on them. Mostly they went walking on the Dales. Sometimes they went to the pictures, nothing to worry about. And I thought Mother was right after all. What good would it do for me to confess and have everything come out."

"But what about Miss Wood?" asked John. "Did she never approach you again about seeing Verity?"

"No, she didn't. She just went ahead and had her to tea, took her into Scarborough twice, shopping. Mother and I were worried, but it looked like she meant it when she said she only wanted to get to know Verity and wouldn't let on about who she was. All the same, I'm going to sort her out about the way she vexed Mother." He looked at his watch. "Plenty of time between now and the five o'clock bus."

John caught himself resenting Nell for taking up some of the time he might have kept Barnes talking—and so increase his own chances for rescue. It was only on second thought that he felt concern for her, and wondered how the little carpenter could be stopped from reaching her. However, apart from the inkpot, nothing occurred to him except to wish, now that he was likely to meet his maker quite soon, that his second thought had been his first.

"I'd almost stopped worrying about Miss Wood," said Barnes, "I was starting to worry so much about young Selkirk and Verity. The two of them were getting too fond of one another if you know what I mean. It's that aircraft spotters' shelter as does it. The Reverend Pigott's preached against it time and again. I'm not saying Verity did anything she shouldn't have, she's not that kind of girl, but still, you have to remember what her mother was, and I couldn't help wondering how long she'd hold out. When he took her to the Budgie Cage, that did it. I didn't care what she knew, I told Verity she wasn't to see him again. I locked her in her room, but of course I had to let her out to go to work, and the next thing I saw Selkirk come from the prop room where'd they'd been meeting after a matinee. I told him to keep away from the lass. A proper lot of lip he gave me too, said we weren't living in the dark ages and Verity was her own woman and entitled to live her own life. And then I saw him, the very next day, up at the shelter again, waiting for her. Well, he couldn't know she wasn't coming. I'd locked her in her room and never mind what she knew. I took my maul and went up to the shelter. He had his back to me, looking at the sunset and smoking that nasty stuff—pot, they call it—and it was as easy as pie. I hit him on the head and he fell over and that was all there was to it. I dragged him into the shelter and went home to my tea, which I couldn't enjoy properly, what with Verity beating on the door and shouting for me to let her out. When it got dark I dragged him down to the disused end of the tip and covered him over with heather branches. T' rats'd take care of him, I thought, and welcome."

John shuddered, thinking of those rats at their work on the pretty boy Ally had loved, while Mr. Barnes calmly went home, released Verity from her room and told her that he had put the fear of God into young Selkirk, who was now on his way back to London. Things had quieted down after that. Verity had sulked for a bit, but it wasn't in her to be disagreeable long, and when on Sunday, mellow with Mrs. Barnes's excellent joint and gooseberry pie, he had said, "He weren't the right kind for you, lass," Verity had hugged her father with tears in her eyes and said, "I know Dad," and they had been friends again.

And then Sir Tancred's dog had found what the rats had left of Tim Selkirk. John wondered whether Barnes planned to "sort out" Sir Tancred and the lurcher as well, but from the way he spoke of him it did not appear that he bore him and Baby any grudge. Tim Selkirk was found, Verity vanished, and the next thing they knew Gaskell turned up at the house to take them to the Scarborough police station where Verity was said to have confessed to both murders. Mrs. Barnes had gone with him, but Barnes, thinking it over and realizing whose fault all this had been in the first place, who had brought both Nell Wood and Tim Selkirk to Rigby, had cleaned and loaded his army revolver and come to sort out John Silk.

"Good God, woman," said Inspector Winterkill to Mrs. Barnes, who was calmly assuring him that her husband would be on the five o'clock bus. "Gone to see Silk at the theater, you say?" He picked up the phone and dialled the Rigby police station. "Who's on duty? Oh, it's you, Troutt, is it? Well, you drop whatever you're doing and hop over to the theater and collect Barnes and bring him in. On what charge? Murder, my lad. Now take the finger out and get cracking. Five o'clock bus indeed."

"I wish you could see it my way, Mr. Silk," said Barnes, sounding friendly and reasonable. "I wouldn't like there to be any hard feelings."

"I'm afraid I really can't," said John, his hand moving stealthily toward the inkwell. "In hiring Miss Wood and Mr. Jagat I did nothing worse than in hiring you and your wife. It seems to me totally unreasonable for you to take this attitude." Were those footsteps in the hallway? Yes, and they seemed to be approaching his door. Now Barnes had heard them too. He lifted his pistol and aimed it at John Silk. The thud of the inkwell flying past Barnes's head and striking the wall, the discharge of the gun, and the opening of the door—all three seemed to happen at the same moment. John felt a tearing pain as he dived for the floor behind his desk. He heard the voice of Mrs. Shrubsole, a sound more welcome than he could ever have imagined, saying stolidly, "That's enough now, Henry," when the lion's-foot leg of the desk seemed to reach out and hit him over the head. Constable Troutt's, "Now then, what is all this?" came from a long way off. Then everything turned black and John Silk ceased to take notice of his surroundings.

CHAPTER XIV

Once more Barnes told his story, this time to the police, but there was no longer any zest in the telling. He was exceedingly tired by the time he had been brought to Scarborough. Just moving his lips to form the twice-rehearsed words was an effort. Mrs. Barnes had been permitted to stay in the room with him. She sat very straight on a wooden chair. He looked at her whenever he felt so fagged that he thought he could not go on. Each time this happened she gave a brief nod, and he continued to talk.

Inspector Winterkill listened to him with the stolid patience he had developed over the years as the most encouraging manner of keeping suspects talking. He never asked questions the first time round. It only distracted the person doing the talking, and sometimes brought him to a dead stop. There would be time to pin down details later.

It could not be said that he was surprised. He thought back to the dead-straight rows of vegetables in Barnes's garden, each spaced the same distance from its neighbor, each the same height as its fellow. Were people who had tidy gardens inclined to be murderers? Did things for them have to be just so? If anything came along to confound the order of their lives, would they pull it up and toss it away, as they would a weed?

Thinking of his own small, untidy garden, he decided that this was a theory flattering to lazy gardeners like himself but not otherwise relevant. Mary Barnes had to have things "just so," but she had not resorted to murder.

She was looking very calm, very composed, was Mary Barnes. The emotions which had spilled over briefly in the prison cell with Verity were tidily put away once more. That was Rigby's way.

The inspector had no doubt that she would stand by Barnes, and do so in the most admirable manner; steadfastly, with never a complaint, and no mention of the disgrace he had brought on his respectable family. Mavis would have been like that too, he thought, and could not help asking himself how Beryl would behave under similar circumstances. The answer came only too promptly. She would cry and carry on, be furious with him for the trouble he was causing her, and show it, come to visit only to heap him with complaints and reproaches, and even that less and less regularly, until the visits ceased entirely, and a letter demanding a divorce would be the last thing he had from her.

Well, what of it? He had no intention of committing a murder. Mavis and Mary Barnes might be splendid creatures in times of adversity, but they hadn't Beryl's long slender legs, and as for Beryl's quickies, you couldn't even think of it without having a laugh. No doubt Beryl was a good-time girl, but he was happy to have her, and if keeping her meant giving her only good times, he would—he decided with the optimism appropriate to a much younger man—see to it that the good times would go on forever.

"So I asked myself," said Barnes, having come to the end of his confession, "who it was had brought all those troubles down on us in the first place, and I went and shot him."

"I do think that most unfair," said John Silk, to whom the inspector was telling this story. "It was Nell who caused all the trouble, not me."

"They're giving him psychiatric tests," said the inspector. "It's a small chance, but it's his only one. 'They were vexing t' missus' isn't a defense that's likely to impress an English jury."

John nodded. In diving behind his desk for shelter he had cracked two ribs, and though he was by now feeling much better, he had got into the habit of being miserly with his breath.

"Sometimes I hate being a policeman, honest," said the inspector. "It's all right, you know, arresting some lout who's coshed an old lady for her pension check. But that dim little chap . . ."

"I can't say I share your feelings," John said crossly. The fact that all of his injuries had been of his own making did nothing to make him think more kindly of the desperate little carpenter. Distracted by the entrance of Mrs. Shrubsole and Constable Troutt, Barnes had missed his aim, and the bullet had passed over John's head and lodged in the wall. But the Victorian monster of a desk had dealt with him instead, a half-open drawer breaking two ribs, and a lion's-claw foot knocking him cold. For a week or so the concussion had made him feel so dizzy and nauseated he had not wanted to see anyone, but since then his recovery had been so unexciting that he was delighted to see Inspector Winterkill and be able to catch up with things that had been happening while he languished, as he romantically put it, on his couch of pain. "To think that I owe my life to Lola Shrubsole," he said. "I shall never get over that."

The inspector laughed. "Neither will she. Lola likes excitement. Another corpse at the theater would have suited her nicely. Oh, I nearly forgot to tell you, Commander Selkirk came to claim Tim's body. He had his two tarts with him, both of them dressed in black vinyl skirts so short they barely covered their sit-down-upons, and high shiny vinyl boots. Apparently their idea of deep mourning."

"No! Do tell me more," said John, starved for the gossip that had been his daily meat and drink at the theater. "What was he like, the Commander? Like the newspaper stories? Poor man, it must have been dreadful for him."

"You couldn't tell it by looking at him. Very much the toff. When I expressed our condolences, he just said, 'Thank you, I didn't know him very well, you know,' and that was that.

His mother didn't bother herself to come for the funeral. She wrote to say that it was her busy season—you'd think she was a termite—and that she didn't see what good it would do her being there."

"She's some kind of an agent for film stars and television people, Tim told me once. I suppose she's right in a way, too. All the same, poor Tim. Not a soul to mourn for him, unless Verity . . ."

"Funny you should mention her," said the inspector, who was sitting by the window. "Here she comes, with Mary Barnes on one side of her and Miss Wood on the other."

John turned cautiously until he too could see out the window. Mrs. Barnes and Nell were weighted down with shopping baskets, but Verity, walking between them, carried nothing heavier than a box which bore the name of one of Scarborough's most expensive dress shops. Lapped in the love of her two mothers, she looked, John thought, distinctly smug. He hated to use the word for such a nice girl, but the look on Verity's face was definitely that of a cat accidentally locked in a well-stocked larder.

"A most unexpected alliance," he said to the inspector.

"Oh, I don't know. They've Verity in common, don't they? They're over at the prison every day. Mary brings Barnes his dinner. Thinks we feed them bread and water, I suppose. Afterwards they all go and have lunch. Lady Biggle offered Mary and Verity jobs at the big house, by the way. She thought they'd be uncomfortable, working at the theater after Barnes tried to shoot you."

"Yes, I know. I do wish she hadn't been so confoundedly feudal about it. I shall never get as good a cleaning woman as Mary Barnes again. And where I'm to find a carpenter who understands the electric wiring I cannot think. Odd, really, people so strictly chapel as the Barneses working in a theater. I've sometimes wondered about that."

"A job's a job, and brass is brass," said the inspector. "Whether it's a theater or a hotel or a hospital doesn't really matter. You pay better wages than a hospital, and we don't have a hotel. I can imagine Mary Barnes making beds in a brothel and never giving it a second thought. Here comes young Beauclerc. Want me to let him in?"

"No, let Mrs. Pinn. She quite fancies him, it's a treat for her."

Gavin stopped by every day, bringing news of the theater, so John knew that Bertie de Grey had appointed himself—without any encouragement whatever from the other actors—its temporary head. In addition, he had given up drinking and was in consequence not merely unpleasant, which they were all used to, but utterly insufferable.

Gavin greeted the inspector and said, "You look very Madame Recamier, reclining on that fainting couch or whatever it's called, Johnny. Oh, Mrs. Pinn, you're an angel, you really shouldn't have bothered." He took the tray with the fresh pot of tea and a plate of hot muffins from her, and put it on a low table, while she stood feasting her eyes and simpering.

"Thanks, Mrs. Pinn, that will be all for now," said John heartlessly. "What's the news at the theater, Gavin?"

"Johnny, how could you?" Gavin said after she had closed the door behind herself. "You know I'm the light of her life." He poured himself a cup of tea and sat down at the foot of John's Madame Recamier sofa. "Well, Bertie's still sober," he said. "It's fifteen days. Do you know the latest fiendish thing he's done? He's gone through all the dressing rooms with a fine-tooth comb, confiscating people's drink, and he tries to stop us going to the pub. I didn't think he could get more abominable, but every day he surpasses even himself."

John laughed cautiously, for deep breaths still hurt his ribs. At the same time, he could not help wondering what was the matter with Gavin. Under the easy flow of talk he seemed for the first time in their acquaintance to be ill at ease. He had drunk his cup of tea, but had not touched the crumpets, which was most unlike him. The inspector, not attuned to these fine shades, made a hearty meal of them instead.

"Anything else?" asked John. "Come along, Gavin, out with it."

Inspector Winterkill looked from one to the other and said he had to be going. "No, really, it's nothing secret," said Gavin so eagerly that John suspected he wanted a third party to act as a buffer. The inspector, suspecting very much the same thing, made his farewells and left.

"Come on, Gavin, let's have it whatever it is."

"Well, it's really quite good news in its way," said Gavin. "Frightfully good news for me, actually. It seems that Sammy was here to watch our *Hamlet*. The night Ally was killed, of all times."

There was a silence, Sammy being a well-known scout for the Royal Shakespeare Company.

John said, "They've offered you a job," and probably only another actor could tell that the warmth he put into this was a piece of very fine acting. Of course he knew that the Rigby Rep was considered a kind of theatrical hatchery, taking in unfledged ducklings and with luck turning them into swans fit for the West End and the RSC. Looked at it in the right way, it was a compliment to the Rigby Rep that they were losing actors to such a prestigious company. But it did not make the losing any easier. "That's splendid news," John said warmly, being far too generous a person to show his true feelings. "I do congratulate you, Gavin. There's no one who deserves it more."

"I shall miss the old Rep, you know that, don't you, Johnny?"

"Not nearly as much as the Rigby Rep will miss you. You'll do us proud, I know."

"It would never have happened without my time here," said Gavin, in a voice that threatened to become emotional, which embarrassed them both. "You look tired, Johnny,"

Gavin added. "All those tea parties are too much for you. I'll go and pester Bertie de Grey."

The afternoon post dropped through the slot in the door. Gavin collected it on his way out and, seeing a letter with the RSC letterhead, slid it to the bottom of the pile before handing it to John.

Left alone, John sorted through his letters, putting aside the bills, slicing his paperknife neatly through the rest, reading them, one after the other, leaving the one from the RSC for last. He knew what it would contain, fulsome compliments on his hatching of thespian swans, and insincere apologies for pinching his most promising young actors. Yet, when at last he made himself open it, it turned out not to be what he expected.

"My dear," it began, "aren't you a dark, *dark* horse," and he could almost hear the emphatic, plummy voice of his old friend Vincent Penford, a voice which could reproduce itself on paper only by double and triple underlinings and freely scattered exclamation points.

When Sammy came back from Rigby he was quite *ahuri*, really, you know, simply slack-jawed with amazement. He said, My dear, did you know Johnny Silk is a *director?* The young chap, Gavin Buckley or whatever he calls himself is brilliant and we *must* have him, but really, you know, good actors are *pebbles* on the beach, while great directors are rarer than good housemaids. Well, I said, Nonsense, Johnny's never directed a thing except the all male chorus line of the Merry Poofters or whatever it was called when we were entertaining the troops back in '42. Well, he's directed *Hamlet,* my dear, said Sammy, and though I said, oh please, Sammy, *nobody* could squeeze one more drop of juice from the *gloomy old thing,* but Sammy said, Well, Johnny's done it, and not gimmicks either, I mean *NOT* Hamlet as a rock star and Ophelia as a groupie, until I agreed to come and see you, though Yorkshire isn't really ME if you know what I mean. As it happened I didn't get to see *Hamlet*, because it was *Earnest* that night, a play nearly as pawed over as our poor old Dane, or don't you agree, and of course Sammy was right, you *can* direct, it was *brilliant!!* Then I was told I couldn't see you because you'd been coshed by the stage carpenter (I had no idea life in Yorkshire was so *exciting!)* and had concussion in the hospital. Well, I had concussion once (remind me to tell you *how* I got it—don't *forget!)* and saw everything double for weeks!! so I thought two of me would be one *de trop*, hence this letter.

The thing is, as I'm sure you'll have guessed, that we want you to come and direct for us. Now don't say No, because we will have great fun and you belong on a *proper* stage (or stages, in our case) not in a place where you get hit on the head and I'm sure you're not appreciated nearly enough.

So do say yes, pretty please. There'll be an official letter, of course, but I wanted to be the first to let you know. Ever *devotedly*, Vinn.

John sat laughing at this familiar voice from the past, and then, as he read the final paragraph a second time, vanity reared its head and shouted "Ha Ha" among the trumpets. The Royal Shakespeare Company wanted him to direct for them—Johnny Silk, who once made a splash as Prince Hal (with Bertie de Grey as a splendid Falstaff), but had never reached the heights predicted for him on the strength of that performance, and had ended in a provincial theater in Yorkshire.

Yet he had been happy here, had enjoyed making the best of his lovely, inconvenient theater, his ducklings and over-the-hill actors, his kiddie matinees on Saturday afternoon, and his old age pensioners and their faithful attendance to whatever was going at reduced rates, to be followed by tea and buns. Even Ally's murder and Barnes's attack on himself had not been able to diminish his affection for the place. After a lifetime of living out of trunks, never settling anywhere long, he had put down roots in Rigby, of all places. Did he want to pull them up again? "No," he said aloud, "certainly not."

And yet, there was the letterhead, Royal Shakespeare Company. Could anyone say no to such an accolade? Could he?

The Cecil Beaton photograph of Ally looked down at him from its place on the chimney piece, but it had no answer for him. The perfect cheekbones were flakes of ash in an urn, while Mrs. Barnes, Nell Wood and Verity walked arm in arm down the High Street. Why couldn't they have shown a little courtesy and shared the girl in the first place? It was as he had said to Tim once, every beastliness, from mayhem on the motorway to nuclear war, is caused by lack of civility. Poor Tim. He was a fairly worthless piece of humanity, he supposed, but he didn't deserve to die and be left to the rats for that.

These were depressing thoughts. To get away from them he read Vinn's letter once more. "You belong on a proper stage, my dear, not in a place where you get hit on the head and people don't appreciate you nearly enough." That was unfair. They did appreciate him here, even if they'd sooner die than show it. He was sure of that. And there was the house on which he had lavished so much money and love. Did he want to leave it behind, to find a rented room somewhere?

"No," he said again, talking to himself as solitary people often do. Still, he didn't have to sell the house. He could come back, spend his holidays here, do some guest directing at the Rep, perhaps. But he knew that if he left he would leave for good. Rigby wasn't the kind of place one visited. It was home or nothing.

All this thinking back and forth was making him tired.

Ever since his concussion he found himself getting sleepy at odd times of day, and dozing off like a cat in a circle of sun on the rug. He closed his eyes. "No," he said once more. "Certainly not." But behind his closed lids he saw, as he drifted into sleep, not his little jewel-box theater in Rigby, but the brick pile in Stratford, overlooking the Avon, Shakespeare's river, flowing gently, bearing its flocks of gracious and greedy swans.